THE UNOFFICIAL
LOLA BAY
FAN CLUB

THE UNOFFICIAL Lola Bay FAN CLUB

C.M. SURRISI

putnam

G.P. PUTNAM'S SONS

G. P. PUTNAM'S SONS
An imprint of Penguin Random House LLC, New York

First published in the United States of America by G. P. Putnam's Sons,
an imprint of Penguin Random House LLC, 2023

Visit us online at penguinrandomhouse.com.

Library of Congress Cataloging-in-Publication Data is available.
Names: Surrisi, C. M., author.
Title: The unofficial Lola Bay Fan Club / C.M. Surrisi.
Description: New York: G. P. Putnam's Sons, 2023. | Summary: "The beginning
of sixth grade brings big friendship changes for Iris, including a new friend
who may not be as good a friend as she seems"—Provided by publisher.
Identifiers: LCCN 2022006910 (print) | LCCN 2022006911 (ebook) |
ISBN 9780593532102 (hardcover) | ISBN 9780593532126 (epub)
Subjects: CYAC: Fan clubs—Fiction. | Friendship—Fiction. |
Middle schools—Fiction. | Schools—Fiction. | LCGFT: Novels.
Classification: LCC PZ7.1.S88 Un 2023 (print) | LCC PZ7.1.S88 (ebook) |
DDC [Fic]—dc23
LC record available at https://lccn.loc.gov/2022006910
LC ebook record available at https://lccn.loc.gov/2022006911

Printed in the United States of America

ISBN 9780593532102
1   3   5   7   9   10   8   6   4   2
BVG

Design by Suki Boynton | Text set in Charter

This book is dedicated to Ellie,
who has embarked upon middle school
with grace and aplomb and has been
my expert consultant.

CONTENTS

THE UNOFFICIAL
LOLA BAY
FAN CLUB

lolabayland NEWS! TOUR STARTING NYC 9/9!! LAST STOP DENVER 11/5!! Click here to see all the stops! 😜 💕 🎸 🎶

1

BEST FRIENDS IN LIFE AND LOLA BAY

THIS WAS OUR most awesome summer.

Every day, Leeza and I packed peanut butter and blueberry jam sandwiches and hung out at the Richfield pool. Some older girls, like Melanie Fisher and her imitators, teased us because we didn't have two-piece bathing suits, but we didn't care.

Like the day Melanie said to me, "Iris, that suit and your wet hair make you look like a third grader. I thought you'd want to know." And Leeza grabbed my arm and said so Melanie could hear, "Ignore her, Iris. At least we *swim* at the swimming pool."

We just didn't let them spoil our fun.

Leeza and I grew up across the street from each other and were total buddies from day one. We played in her sandbox together, hid from her little brothers and sisters in her basement, went to camp and Scouts, and played softball. I liked Scouts and beading bracelets. She liked playing softball and canoeing. Me not so much.

But we both loved the pool. My mom dropped us off, and her mom picked us up, and if we were really lucky, her mom would take us to the bead store or to a movie.

One hot June afternoon, Leeza's mom took us to see the movie *Don't You Dare*. That's when we first saw Lola Bay acting. We'd heard her on KDQB while we were at the pool, and we loved her songs, but since she'd won a Grammy, she was popping up everywhere.

Lola Bay played the part of a girl from a farm who ran away to the city and had to find ways to stay safe. It wasn't easy. She strummed guitar and sang on street corners so people would put dollars in a can by her feet. It was scary. If she hadn't met a really honest social worker lady at a shelter, it could have gone way bad.

We fell in love with her and started watching her online. In her videos she wore a V-neck black T-shirt and super-baggy jeans and had lots of bracelets and rings. Her long hair was pulled up in a messy knot. She wrapped her arms around a big fat acoustic guitar. She sang like Dua Lipa. And she wrote her own songs too, like Billie Eilish. And she growled at the best parts of the song, a little like Lizzo.

Everything else stopped mattering. Lola Bay became our favorite singer—our summer obsession. We sang her songs over and over. We planned to start a fan club when school started, and decorated membership cards.

"And I'm *gone*," I growled.

"Livin' so *strong*," Leeza growled.

We squealed and held hands and jumped up and down.

"This is so rah," Leeza said. *Rah* was her personal multipurpose word. It meant *hurrah, hi ya, big whoop,* or *that sucks*, depending.

"We could be her backup singers," I said. "She's only seventeen, not that much older than us. By the time we're out of high school, she'll still be kind of young."

We downloaded all her songs and played them over and over. We practiced the moves on the videos.

"We have to learn *all* the words to *all* the songs," said Leeza.

"Play that one again," I said. "Did you hear how she came in with the backup singers during part of the harmony?"

We begged our mothers for black T-shirts.

"It has to have a V-neck, Mom!" I cried when she came up to my room saying she'd bought a regular T-shirt.

"I couldn't find a black V-neck T-shirt in your size," she said.

"*Arrrrrrgh!* No, Mom! I need a V-neck!"

"I said they didn't have them." She put the bag down and turned to leave.

"Close my door so Ian and Echo don't come in!" Ian and Echo were my two-and-a-half-year-old twin brother and sister—total tornadoes on toddler feet.

She shook her head and shut the door behind her, saying, "You're welcome."

The bag sat on my desk daring me to open it. A regular T-shirt was just wrong.

Finally, I took it out. The shirt wasn't the worst. I put it on and yanked at the round neck to pull it into a V. A small paper bag with polka-dotted tissue was poking out of the T-shirt bag. When I dumped it out on the bed, four beaded bracelets and a ring with a happy face fell out. They were cool. Very Lola Bay–like.

I sighed. I opened my bedroom door and yelled down the stairs, "THANK YOU FOR THE BRACELETS AND THE RING. I LOVE YOU, MOM." I was not going to thank her for the T-shirt.

I put on my best ripped jeans, the T-shirt, and the jewelry, and checked myself out in the mirror. I tucked part of the shirt into my waistband the way Lola Bay did.

My hair was too short to pile in a knot on the top of my head, but I grabbed a scrunchie out of the drawer and pulled it up into a stubby brown ponytail.

I struck a pose and made pouty lips.

I rummaged for some lip gloss and did it again with more attitude.

I ran downstairs yelling, "I'm going to Leeza's."

In ten seconds, I was across the street. There was no knocking at Leeza's house. I dashed in, took the stairs two at a time, and burst into her room. I tripped over a little kid's toy truck. She was standing in front of her dresser looking in the mirror. She saw my reflection and screamed, "OMG, you look soooo Lola."

"I do?"

"Yes. You look just like her." Then she turned to me. "What do you think?"

I wanted to cry. She had on a black V-neck tee. Her long hair was piled up just like Lola's. She looked beautiful. "You look so perfect," I said.

She held out her bare arm and shrugged. "No bracelets or rings yet, but so what? Right?"

"Right. So what." Then I took off two of my bracelets and gave them to her. "We can trade off on the ring, okay? But I'll get it first because it's mine and everything. Okay?"

She stared at the neck of my shirt. I pulled at it with my fingers.

"We can trade T-shirts too. Okay?"

I hugged her tight, and we stood side by side, looking in her mirror.

"Pose," I said.

"Poutier," she said.

I re-glossed my lips and handed the tube over to her.

She glossed and we posed to Lola Bay's song "Taboo." It was about how being yourself and wanting what you want is okay even if other people say it's wrong. I felt okay about wanting the black V-neck tee, even though my mom said, "You look so nice in bright colors."

✦✦✦

Then the summer ended. It wasn't as if Leeza and I hadn't been obsessing about going to middle school, but I think we'd been hiding our nervousness in Lola Bay. The day before the first day, we had to face it.

We were working on our scrapbook when I had to worry out loud. "It's a super-huge school. What if we get lost?"

"We'll be fine," said Leeza. "We have each other."

That was great, but I was still nervous. "There'll be so many new kids we don't know. It's, like, four elementary schools' worth of sixth graders all dumped together."

"Salima, and Callie, and Bethany, and Paige will be there."

I gripped Leeza's arm. "I hope they'll want to join the Lola Bay Fan Club."

"That would be so great." She shrieked, "We can have epic lip sync contests!"

I jumped up. "We can all listen to the music, and dance, and dress up like her, and do each other's hair. And show them our poses and the scrapbooks, and invite them to make bracelets, and watch movies, and do all the cool stuff we do."

"But it'll be more official," said Leeza, waving a glue stick. "We'll have the membership cards, and maybe we can get a discount on the fan merch page!"

"I didn't think of that before! Wow, we could get discounts on Lola Bay PopSockets!" I spun around. "But what about Melanie and her mean friends?"

"They won't bother us. It's not like at the pool, where they picked on us because they were the queens of the pool. In school we'll just be weenie sixth graders to them. They're seventh graders. They'll be busy with seventh-grade stuff."

I wasn't as confident as Leeza. "Maybe the eighth graders will pick on them," I offered hopefully.

For a minute we both imagined how cool it would be to see eighth graders pick on mean Melanie and her crew. We both sighed big sighs at the same time.

"We'll be fine," said Leeza.

"Absolutely," I agreed even though I wasn't completely convinced. But I had to admit that Melanie might have other things to worry about too.

Then we got lost in deciding what we were going to wear and finishing the Lola Bay Fan Club binder so it would be a work of art. Lola Bay music played the whole time.

I looked at Leeza during a solemn moment in the song "Celebrity." That song was about stepping up and taking the stage. It made me feel powerful. "Can I be president the first year, and then the next year you can be president?"

Leeza made a pouty face, then laughed. "Sure!"

We took turns being onstage on her bed. We planned how the lip sync contests would work and what the prizes would be. When it was time for me to go home, we held hands and promised each other we would be brave in middle school.

✦✧✦

The next morning, we met at the bus stop. My backpack was loaded down with the fat Lola Bay binder. Hers was stuffed with the club notice, our gorgeous handmade membership cards, and clippings. Once we were in our seat on the bus, I said, "Here we go."

She leaned against me. "We'll be fine. Rah?"

This made me laugh. "Rah. We rule."

I clutched my backpack and hummed the Lola Bay song "Livin' So Strong" to myself, and it made me feel mighty.

2

THE LOLA BAY FAN CLUB

I DON'T KNOW why I was so freaked out about the size of the middle school. Our fifth-grade class had toured it in May. Our eighth grader guide, Cinder, had shown us where we'd have homeroom and taken us to the cafeteria, the science lab, the art room, and everything. She'd even told us that in the science lab you could sign up to be a Plant Parent, and the story was that if you kept your plant alive all three years of middle school, you would be a millionaire when you grew up. Leeza thought she could keep a plant alive for three years. I wasn't that confident, but I was pretty sure there were lots of other ways to be a millionaire that didn't involve babysitting a pot of ivy.

Things started to go bad right after we got to our

homeroom. Leeza and I were assigned different advisers, and then we were given different schedules. Our lockers weren't even in the same hallway! Waaaaa! And I'd been assuming we would have that for sure. I wouldn't see Leeza again until lunch. Waaaa! Waaaa!

When the bell rang, Leeza and I squeezed hands. Then we were off to a new world of changing classrooms and finding our lockers. I plowed through a sea of kids. Some I knew, lots I didn't. I kept my eyes and my mind on my schedule and getting to the right rooms. I didn't fully panic until noon, when I looked in the lunchroom. It pulsed with kids carrying trays, yelling to friends, slurping fruity water. The smell almost flipped my stomach. It wasn't totally disgusting, but it didn't smell like any food I could identify. A boy yelled that the Sloppy Joes were horsemeat . . . Yuck.

I stood by the door and searched the chaos for Leeza. I convinced myself that even though my stomach was growling, if I couldn't find her, I would skip eating.

Luck! I saw Callie, Salima, Bethany, and Paige. I could at least sit with them. I threaded through the mass of kids until I reached their table. They were taking their last bites.

"Hi, Iris!" they all said at once.

I hadn't seen them since homeroom. They flooded me with questions.

"Where's your locker?"

"Did you get Mr. Stadler for science? Isn't he nice?"

"Where's Leeza?"

"Are you signing up for any clubs?"

"I can't believe we don't have any classes together!"

I didn't have a chance to answer any of the questions before Leeza showed up at the table with the biggest smile on her face. "Hi, everybody! Isn't this fun?!"

She got a chorus of yeses with the exception of Salima, who seemed to share my feelings about how much fun this really wasn't. I was with Salima. I wasn't so sure yet.

Salima spoke up. "There's going to be lots more homework."

Leeza squeezed in next to me and put her tray down. "Aren't you eating?"

I wanted to scream, *I was waiting for you!* I looked at the lines to the hot food and the cold food and imagined going through them alone. "No, I'm not hungry."

Leeza's eyebrows nearly flew off her face with surprise. "No way." She put a napkin in front of me and started sharing her food. "Here, half of a grilled cheese. Some grapes. Eat."

I was still a little mad, but hungry. I took a bite of the grilled cheese. Then another bite.

"Okay, who's going for a club?" Leeza asked the table.

"I'm going to French Club," said Paige.

"I'm going to Greenies," said Bethany.

"What's that?" I asked.

"Environmental," she replied.

"We're going to Chess Club," said Callie and Salima.

I looked at Leeza and she winked. Then we both launched into telling them about the Lola Bay Fan Club and the cute membership cards, and the lip sync contests, and how much fun it was going to be.

"So, sign up. It meets Thursday," I said. "There will be a room number posted on the club list."

"Sure, that sounds fun," said Callie. "We'll come, won't we?" She looked at the other three in her little gang for agreement.

The other three looked at each other and nodded.

"Yeah, we'll come and see," said Paige.

"Sure. It sounds cool. I like Lola Bay," said Bethany.

✦✧✦

At 2:54 on Thursday, Leeza and I hurried to room 211. I was wearing my horrible regular black tee, but I had on half of my bracelets and the ring. We had our sign-up sheet, cool membership cards, and the binder thick with printouts, clippings, and pictures.

When we peeked into the room, we paused and looked at each other.

I almost backed up and ran. Leeza grabbed my wrist.

Melanie Fisher and the Imitators were at the front of

the room, sitting on the tables. They all wore black V-necks, wrists full of bracelets, and knuckles full of rings.

Callie, Salima, Bethany, and Paige were in the back corner. Callie and Salima sat at a table, and Bethany and Paige leaned against the ledge in front of the window. It was the Spanish room, and the ledge was crowded with maracas, a Guatemalan basket, stacks of comic books in Spanish, and a piñata in the shape of a pencil.

There was one other girl in the room. She sat at a table in the center. Personally, if I was by myself in a room like this, I would not plop myself in the very middle. I would totally sit on the side with my back to the wall.

She looked older than us—a seventh grader? Or maybe even an eighth grader. I'd never seen such brilliantly blue eyes, and the way she leaned back in her chair with her legs crossed said, *I know who I am.* Her black-and-white print dress and dark red suede ankle boots made a perfect combination. Who wore a dress to school? Was that a middle school thing? I looked down at my jeans and black round-neck tee and groaned. I looked so fifth grade.

I couldn't stop staring. Her dark hair was chin length and wavy like my grandma's cocker spaniel's ears. And she had the shortest, straightest bangs I'd ever seen, except maybe on a manga character.

With one arm draped over her backpack, she traced along the zipper with her French-manicured fingertip.

Suddenly she smiled with one side of her mouth, glanced over at Melanie, then looked back to us and rolled her eyes.

Before Leeza and I could get our things unpacked, Melanie Fisher stood up and snapped her fingers. All of her minions turned their heads to her. "Okay, all, let's go around and everyone say their name and something they like about Lola Bay."

My face flushed. What was happening? A cloud of helplessness descended over me. Did clubs have to be run by the oldest kids? Could a seventh grader just take over? I looked to Leeza, and her eyes were shooting fire at Melanie Fisher.

The girl with the cocker spaniel waves called out, "Hold on. I object."

All heads swiveled to stare at her.

Melanie wrinkled her nose. "Oh, great. *Day-na*. Aren't you picture perfect. What?"

"Who put you in charge, *Mel-a-nie*?"

Melanie snickered as if this were hilarious. "Well, Dana. Why don't you start? If you like Lola Bay so much. Say what you like about her."

I held my breath. I'd never seen anyone at the pool

actually pick a fight with Melanie Fisher. All eyes in the room focused on this Dana girl.

She twisted the end of her hair with her perfect fingers. "The sign-up sheet has the names Iris Underwood and Leeza Todd as club founders. You are not Iris Underwood *or* Leeza Todd."

The Imitators sucked air in one collective gasp, then turned to Melanie. We all did.

Melanie Fisher hoisted up a thick turquoise binder with Lola Bay's picture and panned it in front of the group. Lola Bay's face smiled out at us. "For the benefit of you newbie sixth graders, *I* am Melanie Fisher. I'm a seventh grader. *I* am the one who wrote to the Official Lola Bay Fan Club in Los Angeles, California, and *I* am the one who was sent the official chapter registration materials, and *I* have the official membership roster and membership cards. Since the Lola Bay organization has entrusted me with the registration materials, I guess that makes me in charge, and *I* won't sign a card for anyone I don't think deserves to be an official fan."

So much anger welled up inside me, I thought it would blow out my eardrums. My hand hurt from squeezing a pen.

I heard a weak voice in the room say, "I object too."

I realized it was mine. I'd never objected to anything in public before, but there I was, objecting to Melanie

Fisher, because Leeza and I were the ones who'd put up the notice, and *we* were the ones who planned to run the fan club. At the same time, I was kicking myself that I hadn't written for all the official stuff.

"So do I," said Leeza. "I object too."

I looked to the back corner. Salima, Bethany, and Paige were frozen. Callie's face was behind a Spanish comic book.

The flock of Imitator heads all turned to Melanie for her response.

"You see," she started, "this is exactly why I had to come and put a stop to this unofficial meeting. We can't have people pretending to represent the official organization. So, if you sixth graders, and you, Dana Dean, and you girls in the corner want to be in the Official Lola Bay Fan Club . . ." She shrugged one shoulder like it didn't matter to her. "You'll have to follow me. Shall we adjourn to my house, girls?"

With that, Melanie and her gang of official followers got up. Chairs scraped the floor. They whispered among themselves. They snickered. I caught a whiff of their group fragrance as they waltzed out. I glanced at the clock. It was 3:04. Leeza's and my Lola Bay Fan Club had imploded in ten minutes—ten painful, slow-motion minutes.

The Dana girl sat forward and waved her hand. "Honestly. This is no biggie."

I wanted to wail, *What do you mean, no biggie? It's all blown up,* but before I could, she twirled her hair again.

"I'm Dana Dean. I'm in seventh—just like Melanie Fish Face and her gang, and I can tell you, they are losers."

The rest of us in the room spit-laughed when she said Melanie Fish Face.

Dana pulled a thick envelope out of her backpack. It was stuffed with clippings and photocopies that she spread out on the table. Leeza and I had many of the same pictures and printouts in our binder.

Salima, Callie, Bethany, and Paige drifted over to look, but soon said they were leaving to check out other clubs. I wasn't too surprised. You'd have to really, really love Lola Bay to stay after the whole official-unofficial meltdown.

For an hour, the three of us compared our Lola Bay treasures.

"She was only five feet, one inch tall in seventh grade," said Dana.

"Look at this." Leeza pulled out a magazine clipping. "Her hair is actually dark brown."

Manicured fingertips waved a magazine page. "Did you know she sang solos in her high school choir?"

I squealed and pulled out the same picture. "We have that too!"

"She was the third-youngest person to win a Grammy," said Dana.

"And she's sold twenty-five million records since the Grammy," Leeza added.

Then, like it was a secret, Dana tipped her forehead with her straight bangs toward us and whispered, "Can you believe she applied for *American Idol* when she was fourteen and was turned down? How wrong were they! Her influences are Lady Gaga, Ariana Grande, and Sia."

"I don't know about Sia," I admitted.

Leeza shrugged like she didn't know Sia either.

"Sia is really cool. She sang 'Unstoppable.'"

"Oh." I didn't know that song. I thought I knew what Dana had meant when she'd said influences, but I wasn't sure. "What's an influence?"

Dana paused to think for a few seconds. Then she said, "So in the song 'Out of My Way,' Lola Bay sings, 'You can't make me do your thing.'"

Leeza and I nodded.

"It's about knowing who you are, what you want to be, what you can do, in spite of what other people think or expect of you. She probably listened to the Sia song 'Unstoppable,' which is about that, and liked it, and that's where she got the idea."

I was floored. I'd never thought about the words of the songs that way. "Oh my gosh, you are so smart! Thanks for telling us that."

"I get that," Leeza said.

"Sure. My dad is a musician and an artist. They have influences." She looked over the table, and her eyes landed on the membership cards.

The handmade cards that Leeza and I had worked so hard on embarrassed me now with their Sharpie doodles. I said, "You can have one if you want. They're not official. I suppose we'll just throw them away."

Dana's eyes flashed. "Seriously? Who cares about that? If being official means putting up with self-appointed queen bee Melanie Fish Face, I'd rather be unofficial." She sat up straight like she'd surprised herself. "Hey, let's be unofficial."

I laughed. I was stunned she wanted to be unofficial with us. "Really?"

"Sure. Lola Bay would hate Melanie Fish Face. I think the real Lola Bay—not her publicity, computer, plastic people—would rather be unofficial with us if she had the chance."

"You do?" Leeza asked.

"Absolutely." Dana picked up one of the cards that Leeza had made. One with silver stars.

Her hands were so pretty. I'd never really noticed hands before—anybody's hands, really. She had long slender fingers. She noticed me looking at them as she wrote her name. "I'm going to be a hand model when I grow up."

"You are?" asked Leeza.

"Cool," I said. Of course! That seemed like an obvious thing for her to do. She was so smart and confident. Still, I couldn't understand why a seventh grader would want to hang out with us. "You know we're only in sixth grade."

"I was once too," she said. "I don't really have friends in my grade, or at school, really. I'm very picky about who my friends are. But I adore Lola Bay. She's worth fanning over. I don't care if you're in sixth grade or high school if we really have that in common."

"Really?"

"Well, maybe that high school thing is an exaggeration. I'm not sure a high school kid would hang with us."

We all laughed.

"Sure. That would be cool. We could eat lunch together," I offered.

"Whoa. Uh, that might be too much."

"Okay. Right," I said.

"But I could come over to your house after school sometime, and we could listen to her music and watch her videos. You have a computer, don't you?"

"Oh yeah. I have a laptop."

"In your room?"

"Uh-huh."

She nodded like she was impressed, and gave me a thumbs-up.

"When do you want to come over?" I asked.

"Soon," she said.

"That will be so much fun," said Leeza.

So much for Melanie Fish Face and the Imitators. Dana and Leeza and I would be better off unofficial. We'd have lots of fun listening to Lola Bay music and talking about influences.

We got up to leave and Dana said, "Here." She pulled a black wad out of her backpack and handed it to me. "I think you need this."

I unrolled it. It was a V-neck. My eyes bugged. "Wow, thanks. That's really nice. Are you sure?"

"Yes. I have, like, four more. I brought it to talk about whether we should have them printed with a local club emblem."

I almost teared up. This totally cool seventh-grade girl wanted to be unofficial with us, and she gave me a black V-neck tee, and she told us about influences, and she had the best idea ever to print a local club emblem on shirts. Melanie Fish Face seriously didn't matter.

"So do you want to come over tomorrow?" I asked. I still couldn't believe it.

"Sure," said Dana.

"Okay!" Leeza said. "That's great. Do you want to ride the bus home with us?"

Dana smiled her half smile. "Uh, no. Just give me the address."

I wrote it down. As we left the room, I felt an over-whelming gush of happiness. I turned to Leeza and said, "That was so much fun."

Leeza laughed and threw her arm around my neck. "I can't say I'd call it *all* fun, but middle school isn't so bad, is it?"

"Do you want to do manicures when we get home?" I asked her.

"Oh yeah. Do you think we can do French like Dana?"

"I can do yours and you can do mine." I looked at my nails. They were stubby short. "I have to stop biting my nails so they'll grow."

Leeza laughed. "At least so I can put a skinny white line there."

We may not have had all the official stuff, but we had a cool new friend who seriously liked Lola Bay, was really smart, and didn't mind hanging out with sixth graders. I started to think this might actually be a good year. And my nails were going to look better.

3

AN OFFICIAL BOND

THAT WAS THE beginning of the Unofficial Lola Bay Fan Club. Dana Dean, Leeza Todd, and Iris Underwood. Melanie Fish Face, as we now regularly called her, went around school and told everyone we were breaking the official club rules and that we were loser sixth graders hanging out on the dark side with weird Dana Dean.

Dana was different from anyone I had ever met before, but I wouldn't have called her weird. The day after we became the unofficial club, she came over to my house, and Leeza and I sat at her feet in my room while she told us that Melanie Fish Face was jealous of her.

"She can't bully me, and she knows it," Dana said.

"We have history. I have my little ways of getting my satisfaction."

Leeza and I were all ears.

"What?" asked Leeza.

"How?" I asked.

"Oh, let's just say I'm smarter than she is."

That was all she would give us on the Melanie Fish Face situation. Dana was full of information about other kids in school, like Jeremy Melborne, who was to be avoided because he was a major nose picker, and some of the teachers too, like Ms. Ochs, who was a champion clog dancer on the weekends. We memorized it all for future reference. But mostly, she was wise about Lola Bay. And she could talk forever about music, musicians, and art.

One day at school, we were walking down the hall toward art class, and she pulled me aside.

"Iris, come here. Put these ear pods in."

Her phone was loaded with Lola Bay music.

I had a phone, but I had to keep it turned off at school and only use it for emergencies.

She cued up "Blue Sky." "Lola Bay wrote this when she was ten," Dana explained. "After she had her first hit, the record people asked her if she had any old songs, and she showed them this one and they did a new arrangement for her."

I had a vague idea that an arrangement had something to do with how you sang the song. She must have seen the question in my eyes.

"You know how in an arrangement they figure out the best key and timing for the song and what the harmonies will be and all that? Well, they also made her change some of the lyrics because they were too little-kiddie."

"Oh yeah, I can see how they would do that." I marveled again at how smart Dana was about Lola Bay, and music arrangements, and lots of other stuff. Then I remembered her dad was a musician.

By the end of the second week of school, she had been to my house three times and the Unofficial Lola Bay Fan Club was crazy busy collecting photographs, writing up career timelines, and designing scrapbook pages. We'd known her one week and we were learning so much. I did kind of care that people thought we were on the dark side, but not that much. We were having so much fun.

Then one morning at the bus stop Leeza said, "I'm not coming to fan club after school."

I was stunned. "What! Why?"

"I'm trying out for volleyball."

"Is this about kids saying we're on the dark side?"

She laughed. "I don't care about that. I just want to play volleyball. That's okay, isn't it?" She raised her eyebrows at me.

My breath caught in my throat. "But . . . but you'll come back, right?"

The bus arrived and the driver opened the door. Leeza started moving, but I grabbed her sleeve. "You're not quitting the club, are you?"

She pulled away. "No. I guess not. But maybe. It's getting boring—for me." She turned and jumped on.

I fell into our seat next to her. "Why is it boring? Don't you like Lola Bay anymore?"

She shrugged and turned to stare out the window at the houses going by. The kids in the front seat pulled each other's hair and had a slap fight.

"What? Tell me!" This stung me like a paper cut. "Don't you love Lola Bay anymore?"

She turned back toward me. "I still *like* her, but, you know, there's so much other stuff to do. You can still do your fan club and everything with *Day*-na."

I hardly knew what to say. First of all, she *was* being a little mean to say that. And second, how could she just stop loving Lola Bay? I mean, how does a person just stop loving someone, like, *snap*?

"I'll switch with you next year, so you can be president,"

I offered. But at the same time, I knew it wasn't Lola Bay.

It was Dana.

She didn't like her as much as I did. She didn't like listening to her tell us music stuff. She'd been zoning out when Dana did this. I'd seen it, but I'd stuffed it down.

Leeza looked at me like she had a lot on her mind, but only said, "There's just so much more to do. You know me. I like sports. I really want to play volleyball."

The bus bumped over a railroad track, and we were jostled in our seat. "Is this about Dana?"

"Maybe a little."

My heart was in my throat and I knew if I said much more, I'd cry. We were quiet until the bus pulled into line in front of school. When the door opened, I said, "You are my best friend, you know that. Not Dana."

She looked a little sorry, but she said, "I still like Lola Bay and all, Iris, but I want to play volleyball and do some other stuff." There was something about the way she said "Iris" that felt like she'd taken two steps back from me. She must have seen the hurt on my face, because she gave me a quick hug and added, "It's okay, rah. We can do lots of other stuff together. You can have my black V-neck if you want."

She leaned against me. "It's okay to have more than one good friend. We're cool."

I smiled with half my mouth. Then I realized I was mimicking Dana. Bad move.

Leeza rolled her eyes.

✦ ✧ ✦

The lump in my throat was still stuck there during Studio Arts. It was usually my favorite class, especially since it was the one class I had with Dana. But I grumped all the way through it.

As we walked out, Dana asked, "What's up with you?"

I muttered, "Nothing."

"Are we still meeting tomorrow?"

"Uh-huh."

"Okay, I'll come over."

"Good."

On the bus, my mind whirled with memories of me and Leeza. The more good times I remembered, the hotter my face burned. I put my cheek against the cool window.

As I walked home from the bus stop, I kicked the low bushes along the sidewalk. The joy of the Unofficial Lola Bay Fan Club was fading with every step. Okay. I *did* want Leeza's V-neck. I had the one Dana had given me, but it never hurt to have two. But it didn't make up for her giving up on Lola Bay.

I felt like I was carrying a full bucket of water all the way home and it could spill at any second. When I walked into the house and saw my mom standing by the kitchen sink, the bucket tipped, and the tears splashed.

"Oh my gosh, Iris, what's the matter?" She rushed to me. "Are you okay? What happened?"

I choked out the word. "Nothing."

Mom grabbed a dish towel and handed it to me as I turned to head up to my room.

She called after me, "It doesn't look like nothing."

"It's nothing!" I yelled.

"Well, I'm here if you want to talk."

"I DON'T! And don't let the twins come in my room!" I slammed my door.

What did she know? She couldn't even find a black V-neck T-shirt to buy.

I flopped on the bed and mumbled to myself. "I hate sports. I don't want to play stupid volleyball." I pulled the neck of my shirt up over my nose into my thinking position. For one second, I was glad it was the green one so I could get it all the way up over my face.

I wondered what Lola Bay would do if this happened to her. But of course, nothing like this would ever happen to her. She was perfect and probably had perfect friends who never let her down.

I jammed in my earbuds and listened to my favorite

Lola Bay album, *Misty Me*. Her voice rolled over me like bubbles in a warm bath. "Livin' So Strong," "Out of My Way," "I Do Me," "Bluebird Wing Tip." I adored "Bluebird Wing Tip." I sang along. "Slicing through the mist you make, I know where I am landing."

✦ ✦ ✦

By the next week, Leeza was deep into playing volleyball and watching the boys' track meets. She had no time for me. Maybe it would be fairer to say we had less time for each other.

"Rah," Leeza said when I met her one morning at the corner.

"Rah," I answered.

We claimed our seat on the bus.

"How's volleyball?"

"Good. Regina— You know Regina, right?"

"From volleyball? Uh-huh."

"Regina says she thinks Ted is in love with me."

Her eyes shone with excitement. I wanted to be thrilled for her, but I just couldn't. "That's good."

Leeza rolled her eyes. "Rah, Iris. Yes, that's good."

"That's what I said!"

Leeza leaned over and whispered to me, "Regina called you a fan-geek. I thought you should know. I didn't agree or anything even close to that. I told her to shut up."

I imagined Regina pointing at my back and saying, *Fan-geek!*

"Leeza! I'm a fangirl, not a geek! I'm a Lola Bay F-A-N."

"Fan her, geek her, nerd her, whatever. I told Regina to shut up."

We rode on to school and I thought, *I'm glad I have Dana as a fangirl friend.* I didn't really need Leeza to defend me, but it was cool of her.

LOLA BAY ENDURES

WHEN DANA WALKED into my room, she was very serious.

"Ahem. May I be recognized?" she asked.

"Sure," I answered. I had no idea what was going on.

"I, Dana Dean, full-fledged member of the Unofficial Lola Bay Fan Club, hereby nominate Iris Underwood, also a full-fledged member of the Unofficial Lola Bay Fan Club, as president of such club."

The words settled in my ears and a thrill rose in me. I sat up straight.

She leaned over and whispered, "You have to second the nomination, because you are the only other member."

It was true. We'd tried to recruit Callie, Paige, Bethany, and Salima with no success. I said, "I second the nomination."

"All in favor, say aye," said Dana.

"Aye," we both said.

Then she took the ruler off my desk and tapped me on each shoulder like she was the queen of England and I was a knight, and she slipped a cool bracelet off her wrist and onto mine. Then she said, "I pronounce you president!"

I just knew that Melanie Fish Face hadn't had such a cool coronation.

I admired my wrist in the mirror while Dana went over to the computer.

She was so fast. Click. Click. Click. As she searched the internet for articles, I played with the beads on my new bracelets. Then she printed pages and I filled up scrapbooks.

That Friday, I was making a bracelet and telling Dana about how Melanie Fish Face and the Imitators had snickered at me in the hall, which had hurt my feelings for the hundredth time. As I was talking, she magically made a colorful spreadsheet on my computer. It had columns for record titles, record sales, movie titles, box office receipts, and concert cities and dates. Then she opened websites and started copying and pasting things into it.

"How do you know how to do that?" I asked her.

"I taught myself." Click. Click. "I could show you how."

"Huh." I really wasn't that interested in making a spreadsheet. Anyway, she knew how to do it, so that was good enough.

"Look at this," she said, pointing to a link at the bottom of the site. She clicked on it, and all kinds of things popped up that I didn't understand. She scrolled up and down, nodding.

"What's that?"

"It's the webmaster's door."

"Can you open it?"

"Nope. It's locked."

Dana moved on to our school library site and opened it. "Hey, what's your e-library password?" Her hands paused over the keyboard as the cursor blinked in the window.

"Why?"

"Just give it to me, silly."

"UnderwoodI1798."

She entered my password, opened the portal, and somehow navigated to a page with the student list. She highlighted Melanie Fish Face's student ID, and then started checking out books. It happened so fast, my eyes could barely keep up. Dana checked out a book on puberty. Then another. Then another. Then another. Until it looked like Melanie had all the books on getting your period, hormones, and understanding human sexuality.

"Oh my gosh!" I had my hands over my mouth covering a scream. "Won't she know you did that?"

"Nope. It will look like she checked them out."

"But where are the books?"

"Still on the shelf."

"How did you do that?"

"What can I say? I'm a genius."

"When will she find out?"

"When she gets the overdue notices—or when someone else tries to check one of them out, and they can't because it looks like it's checked out to her and she gets called in."

"This is so, so hilarious!" I laughed. But secretly I wished she'd used her own account number. I didn't want to get caught pulling a prank on Melanie Fish Face.

"Come on," she said, like that fun was over. "Let's put our new Lola Bay printouts into the scrapbooks."

✦✧✦

We'd spent a lot of afternoons up in my room, with Dana surfing on my computer and me putting things in the scrapbooks. Sometimes, Dana would go back to the Lola Bay webmaster's door to try to guess the password.

One day near the end of the month, I asked her, "Why are you doing that?"

"I don't know. Because it's fun." She shrugged. "And if I figure it out and get through the paywall, you can sometimes get free stuff."

"Like what?"

"You know, things like posters."

We also watched a ton of Lola Bay videos on YouTube and sang our heads off. Dana had a really good voice. She could make herself sound just like Lola Bay. We tried watching concert clips on the big TV downstairs, but our family room looked like a day care center with piles of toys, board books, blocks, and puzzles. The furniture was all a little sticky and smelled like graham crackers, and every time we went in there, the twins tried to sing along, so we couldn't hear a thing.

I wanted to go to Dana's house sometimes, but she always said, "We can't. My dad works nights and sleeps days, and the house has to be quiet." I could understand that. Still, I wanted to see her room and the giant Lola Bay posters she talked about.

My mom wanted to know more about her too. She'd been asking questions off and on and getting short little answers that I knew didn't satisfy her. Then one day, when we were about to hurry upstairs to watch the big release of a new Lola Bay video, Mom decided to go all police detective on Dana.

Over oatmeal cookies, Mom cross-examined her. "So, Dana. Where do you live?" "I'd like to meet your parents." "What are their names?" "What does your father do?" "What does your mother do?" It was so embarrassing.

Dana gave her the same answers she gave me. "My dad works nights and sleeps days, so he's hard to meet, and my mom works days and sleeps nights. He's a musician and a metal artist. He's in a collective with some other artists in North Minneapolis. My mom is a psychologist at the University of Minnesota Medical Center."

Mom's eyebrows arched. "Oh, that's nice."

I groaned. She was all impressed that Mrs. Dean was a psychologist.

She started fixing a snack for the twins, who were throwing toys in the other room, but she wasn't done. "Does she like working at the university?"

Dana picked a raisin out of a cookie. "Duh. I have no idea."

My mother spun around and looked at her. Her gaze lingered a second on Dana's French-tipped fingernails holding the raisin.

Dana checked herself. "I could ask and let you know."

Mom gave her a half smile. "So where do you live?"

Dana sighed like it was not really our business. "At 273 Forsythia Lane."

At dinner that night, Mom wouldn't let it go.

"Iris's new friend is interesting," she said, reaching back and forth from the counter, putting dishes in front of us.

Dad struggled to get Ian in his high chair, and I wrestled with Echo. They were all arms and legs when it was time to eat, kicking chairs and tossing apple slices with screams of joy. Once they were settled, they were adorable. Like eager puppies.

"Oh yeah?" He turned his attention to squirting mustard onto his hot dog. "Are these the ones from that butcher shop in New Prague?"

"Yep. These are the last of them. We'll have to take a ride down there and get some more." Mom slid a bowl of macaroni salad across the table. "Yes. I got to know Dana a little better today."

"This is the girl with the short bangs?" Dad asked me through a bite of hot dog.

"Yes, we are the Unofficial Lola Bay Fan Club. You *know* this."

He was in humor mode. "Okay. Okay. Calm down. Don't get your undies in a bundle. It's our job to know who your friends are."

I groaned.

Sunday afternoon, the twin racket in the house was at Disney World level, so Mom suggested I go hang out with Leeza. It didn't take me two seconds to reject that idea. Her house was noisier than ours and I wasn't sure what we'd do, so I decided to go to Dana's instead. I wanted to see her room and maybe meet her artist dad. So I pedaled to Forsythia Lane.

The street curved alongside the lake. The houses all had big old trees that arched over their driveways. I stopped by the mailbox with 273 on it. The house was big and white and had lots of windows. A beat-up old pickup angled its nose into one of the garage doors, and a silver sedan pointed toward the other.

I was about to ride up the driveway and ring the doorbell when the front door flew open and a woman dressed in bright workout clothes barreled out.

"Let's go, Dana. Get a move on," she called.

Dana called from inside the house, "I don't want to work out in a gym. I am fine doing yoga at home."

It didn't seem like a good time to introduce myself.

I backed up behind a bank of lilac bushes and watched.

"Come on!" her mom yelled.

Instead of her usual perfect dress and boots, Dana appeared in pink-and-gray yoga clothes. "I don't want to."

Her mom opened the car door. "You really have to learn to compartmentalize your negative feelings. Not everything in life is the way you want it to be. Besides, mother-daughter events are good for mind and body." She got in, and in seconds the car jumped to life.

Dana rolled her eyes and pouted her way to the passenger side of the car. Then she planted her feet and folded her arms.

Her mom powered down the window. "Get in the car now."

I slunk back farther into the leaves and held my breath, waiting to see how this standoff would end. Would her mom get out of the car and force her in? Would Dana run back into the house?

"I hate sweating. I hate you!"

Her mom leaned across the seat and barked, "I have a professional reputation to uphold at the medical center. Do you understand? This is a mother-daughter event for the Hospital Guild. Now get in the damn car."

Dana yanked open the car door with a vengeance. "Fine, but I want a Monkey Don donut after."

"Fine."

"Promise."

"Yes. I promise. I'll get you a Monkey Don donut if you get into the car and behave yourself at the gym."

Dana slammed the door, and the car flew out of the driveway and into the street without even slowing down. I ducked deeper into the bushes. A branch poked my neck and my heart nearly stopped.

As they pulled away, I shivered. My mom had never talked to me that way, and I'd never said something like that to her. I mean, I got mad at my mom and yelled at her sometimes, but I didn't *hate* her. The echo of the word *hate* made me pump my bike hard on the way home. But I was also wondering about Monkey Don donuts. Where did you get them? They must be really good.

5

THE IN-BETWEEN

MONDAY MORNING, I climbed on the bus still thinking about the scene in Dana's driveway and wondering about Monkey Don donuts.

Leeza ran to the bus and jumped on, barely squeezing through the closing door. She slammed into me as she hit the seat. "Rah. Made it!" It was good old Leeza. Her cheeks were rosy from running. "Hey. How was your weekend?"

"Good." I briefly thought about telling her what I had seen at Dana's house, but I stopped. That was too personal to share with someone who didn't know her very well. "How was yours?"

"Great. Had volleyball camp on Saturday morning and watched the boys' track practice in the afternoon."

"Oh yeah? How was that?" I leaned into her shoulder and smiled.

She blushed. "Stop!"

"Who were you *watch*-watching?"

Leeza wrapped her arms around her backpack. "You know. Ted. He's nice. I think I might be in love with him." She was serious as a math test.

I thought I did great by not pretending to barf. Ted Eckles was skinny, had a face full of pimples, and spoke in three-word sentences. I couldn't help imitating how he talks, though. "Uh. Yeah. Sure."

She said, "Shut up," but she smiled.

We rode in silence for a while. Other kids yelled and threw wads of paper, and the bus driver yelled, "Quiet down!"

Leeza zipped and unzipped the top pocket of her backpack. "I know you think he's geeky. But I think he's just shy. You must like someone."

Somehow, thankfully, we were pulling up at school and I didn't have to say any more about Ted Eckles or answer the question about who I liked. No boy interested me more than the Unofficial Lola Bay Fan Club.

After lunch, as I was walking to Studio Arts, I turned

a corner and nearly ran into Leeza. She had her arm linked with Regina's, and their heads were close. They were laughing like one of them had just said the funniest thing ever. At first, I thought Leeza would look up and see me and say "Rah," but she didn't. So I glanced away like I didn't see them either, because for some stupid reason, I was starting to choke up. I breathed through the tightness in my throat until I was perched on a stool in the corner with my easel pulled back as far as possible so no one could see my work. From this spot I could draw a manga version of Lola Bay without anyone bugging me.

Dana sat on the other side of the room. Today she was popping her head out from behind her easel and making goofy faces to make me laugh. She'd look first to see if anyone else was watching. They never were.

I guess having a fight with her mom was no big deal. I wondered if she had gotten her Monkey Don donuts.

"May I see?" Ms. Wells startled me. She was practically on top of my easel. She liked to talk about my work and really, really look at it.

"I guess."

She studied my newest version of Lola Bay with giant eyes. "Your favorite subject." She smiled. Not phony or sarcastic.

I relaxed. "I know."

"I like your passion. What are you going for in the piece?"

I didn't think I was going for anything. "It's a manga version."

"Sometimes we surprise ourselves," she said.

"I guess."

"Creating art is discovering something we already know deep inside. That's what artists do. They art-it-out."

For a second, I wondered what deep thought was already inside me about Lola Bay, but my question was crowded aside by the realization that Ms. Wells had called me an artist.

Then I caught Dana looking at me. When we locked eyes, she crossed hers. I laughed. It convinced me she hadn't seen me by her driveway the day before. I waited until she looked away and asked, "Ms. Wells, do you have influences?"

She cocked her head like she wasn't sure what I meant. "Do you mean artistic influences?"

I glanced to be sure Dana wasn't watching. I wasn't sure why, but I felt like I was checking on what she had told me about influences. "Yes. Like what an artist has."

Ms. Wells smiled. "Sure. Like you. You are influenced by the manga style."

It was like, duh. Of course. I knew that.

"Come on. I have a great idea," Dana said as she hurried up to my room that afternoon.

I raced up the stairs after her. "What?"

She dumped a fistful of cards on the bed. "Get pens!"

"What are we doing?" I wanted to know.

She held up one of the cards like it was something she was showing in a commercial. "These are subscription cards to magazines. *House Beautiful, Road and Track, Fin and Feather* . . ." She shuffled through a few more. "*National Geographic, Puppeteer, Amateur Radio—*"

"What for?"

"Duh, we're subscribing."

"I don't like any of these magazines, except maybe *Puppeteer* sounds cool."

"Not for us, dodo. For Melanie Fisher." Dana positively shivered with excitement.

I was not down for this at all, and I was kind of losing interest in the whole punish-Melanie-Fish-Face thing. "What's the deal with you and Melanie Fish Face?"

Her perfect face fell. A cloud stirred behind her eyes. I got a little scared that she was going to leave when she scooped up all the subscription cards and tapped them into a neat stack. When she was done, she tipped her head down and looked at me under knitted eyebrows. Her bangs were in their perfect straight row like always.

"Iris, do you think you're my friend?"

The back of my neck tensed. I wasn't sure if she was asking me to say yes or trying to tell me we were just two girls who both liked Lola Bay.

But I really thought we *were* friends, so I said, "Yes. I think we're friends." And I held my breath, wishing I'd never asked about Melanie Fish Face.

Her face softened and she whispered, "I think so too. And if you really are my true friend, I will tell you what Melanie Fisher did to me."

Relief flooded through me along with a desperate urgency to know. I whispered back, "You can trust me. I won't tell anyone."

Dana sat on my bed and leaned against the headboard. "*Can* I trust you?"

"Yes," I said in my best solemn promise voice. I sat down by her feet.

"I thought I could trust her too."

"I would never betray you," I said with all my passion. "We are sisters in Lola Bay. We are the founders of the Unofficial Lola Bay Fan Club. I mean, what are friends for?"

She looked toward the door as if checking to be sure it was closed good and solid.

"So," she said, trailing a manicured fingertip along the quilt line of the bedspread. "Melanie and I were like you and Leeza. We'd been friends forever, always just us two.

She was always wanting to do wild stuff, like sneak out our bedroom windows at night to catch fireflies, dig in our mothers' makeup bags and try their lipsticks, things like that. And I was, I guess, okay with it. Then it was the summer after third grade, and she said the school was open and we should go in there and run around and do anything we wanted. Like roller-skate down the halls or whatever."

I imagined roller-skating in an empty school, and it sounded super-fun.

"So we went to the school, and inside the front door there was a chair and a clipboard and a pen but no person to ask us any questions. They must have been in the bathroom or something. We ran in and raced down the halls—no roller skates—and tried the classroom doors along the way. And one was unlocked."

"Oh, wow. Which room was it?" I instantly imagined having the art room all to myself.

"It was Ms. Spinelli's room. She was one of the fourth-grade teachers we knew we could have when school started. Melanie ran to her desk and started opening the drawers. She took a lot of stuff out, and she showed me a little stack of photographs that were in the pencil drawer. They were of some baby. Probably Ms. Spinelli's baby. I didn't know. Then Melanie picked up a stapler and stapled all over the baby's face in all the pictures. I kept telling her to stop it. And then she pulled a metal box with flowers painted on it out of a drawer, and when she opened it, lots of quarters fell out. She stuffed a bunch in her pocket."

My mouth must have been hanging open. I couldn't stop feeling like I was there, in the room, watching Melanie be such a devil.

"Then we heard the janitor turn on the floor-waxing machine and Melanie screamed, 'Let's go!' and we ran like crazy out the back door of the school."

"What happened then?" This was like the best TV show ever.

"What happened was that the school had cameras in the hallways, and the principal called our parents and Melanie Fish-Face-Awful-Horrid-Creep said it was my idea, and that I'd stapled the baby pictures and I'd taken the quarters."

"OH MY GOSH. What did you do?"

"Her parents said they absolutely believed her and would sue the school if they blamed Melanie. My mom didn't stand up for me. Even though I swore a million times on my life that it wasn't me. She kept saying, 'What the heck were you doing in the school anyway?'"

"What happened?"

"I kept saying it wasn't me, and Melanie kept saying it was me, and the principal said there was no way to know who was lying, but he wasn't going to get the school sued over it. So he made us both apologize for being at the school, and then he put us both in Ms. Spinelli's class in fourth grade."

"That must have been awful."

"That's not all. Melanie brought Ms. Spinelli presents, and her parents gave a big donation for the fourth-grade class trip. And she told *everyone* it was me and that I made her go in the school and I was even laughing when I stapled the baby's face."

I could barely believe what I was hearing. "What did Ms. Spinelli do?"

"She was okay. I kind of think she knew it wasn't me, but I was never sure. Sometimes she took the pictures out of her drawer with the holes where the staples used to be and got kind of weepy."

"Did your parents do anything?"

"My mom said I needed to compartmentalize it and move on. My dad was nice. He said if Melanie ever came to our house again, he'd throw a bucket of paint on her."

I didn't know what to say. My head was swimming with the idea that Melanie had lied so bad. Poor Dana. I studied her in amazement. In spite of this horrible thing that Melanie Fish Face had done, Dana still looked the same: elegant, composed, and in control.

"Wow." That was all I could say.

"So do you still wonder why I always want to do stuff to make her life miserable?"

I reached across the bed and gave her a hug. Then I put out my hand and she gave me half the stack of magazine subscription forms. We put on Lola Bay's second album, *Spark and Spunk*, and spent the next hour writing Melanie Fisher's name and address on the magazine subscription cards and checking the box that said "BILL ME."

"I don't think we should send her *Puppeteer*," I said.

"Why not?" Dana asked.

"Because it sounds like too good of a magazine for her."

"Yeah. You're probably right."

Then I remembered something. "Is that why she said you were picture perfect at the first club meeting?"

"Bingo."

When Mom called me for dinner, Dana got up and said, "Tomorrow after school, do you want to come to my house?"

REAL FRIENDS

THAT NIGHT I couldn't sleep, thinking about the baby pictures full of pinpoint stabs. Not just the holes, but Melanie actually stapling them. It felt so violent. It was like it hurt the baby. It hurt me. It must have hurt Dana, being right there and all. And the idea of Ms. Spinelli carefully taking out each staple and having to look at the marred face. It just haunted me. It made me willing to do meaner things to Melanie Fish Face.

Knowing this story made me feel closer to Dana. So when I went home with her after school the next day, I was prepared for a cruel prank on Melanie Fish Face. But Dana didn't have one planned.

When we got to her house, it was locked up tight.

She took out the key and slipped it into the lock. As she turned it, she said, "Shhhh. My dad is probably sleeping."

But when we were inside and she closed the door behind us, I heard a man's voice. "Dana? That you?"

"Yes, Dad. It's me and Iris."

"Who's Iris?" This was followed by some plinks on strings.

"Iris Underwood."

"That doesn't tell me much. Bring Iris Underwood up here." Plink. Plink.

This made me nervous for two reasons. One, it was like a command to be examined to see if I was good enough to be her friend. And two, why had she never mentioned me to her dad before? We hesitated by the door. There were stairs going up and stairs going down. She threw her backpack downstairs and pointed for me to do the same, and then we walked up.

"He won't throw a bucket of paint on you," she said. "I don't know why he's not sleeping."

"Iris is my best friend," Dana said as she rounded the corner into the kitchen.

A thin man in jeans and a paint-splattered T-shirt was sitting with one leg crossed over the other, holding a small instrument that looked like it was half guitar, half violin. He cradled it like a baby. His face was tipped down and his fingers plucked the strings, making tinny sounds.

"What's that?" I surprised myself when I blurted that out, but then again, I was now Dana's best friend.

"Tell her," he said without looking up.

She opened a cupboard and took down two mugs. "It's a mandolin."

Suddenly, the plinks erupted into music and Dana's dad's fingers were picking and slapping and pulling the peppiest sounds out of the funny little instrument. His foot tapped and his head bobbed. With his eyes closed, he went off into another world while Dana filled a teapot with boiling water from the hot water dispenser and popped in four tea bags and three spoonfuls of sugar all at once.

"Grab the mugs," Dana said. She picked up the teapot and a package of Lorna Doone cookies, ignoring the mini-concert going on in her kitchen.

I did as I was told and followed her. It seemed rude to leave while her dad was playing, so I hesitated. She turned and said, "He's gone. Let's go."

We went down to the lower level, and when she opened the door to her room, I immediately got smacked in the eyes by two unbelievable Lola Bay posters. They were the size of bedsheets and framed in white against cocoa-colored walls. It was like an art gallery. One poster was from her first tour, Courtly, and the second was from her movie, *Last Tomorrow*. I didn't know they made posters that big. Dana must have seen my mouth hanging open.

"They're for movie theaters and stadiums."

"How did you get them?"

She tipped her head. "Well . . . that little back door to the website."

"Wow. I had no idea."

She moved a stack of books, put the teapot on her desk, and tossed the Lorna Doones to me. "Do you like these? They're my favs."

I couldn't remember if I'd had them or not, but since we were best friends now . . . I supposed they could be my favorite. "Yes. I like them."

She connected her phone to a speaker and played Lola Bay's *High Water* album.

"Do you like mint tea?"

I'd never had mint tea. "Sure. I love it."

Dana kicked off her ankle boots and poured two steamy cups. We sat on her floor on a fluffy rug, sipped tea, and ate Lorna Doones.

She held a cookie with her fingertips. "I think mint tea and Lorna Doones will be our secret snack."

"I love that." I was glad I could say I loved Lorna Doones, because if the cookies had had coconut in them, it would have been a problem. Yuck to coconut in cookies. Or anything, really.

"We won't tell anyone."

"No one."

We listened to one track after another. The richness of Lola Bay's voice filled the room. Soon we were singing along. Then we were up and dancing.

Suddenly, Dana shut the music off and posed with her fingertip at her chin. "I have a fabulous idea."

"What?"

"I'm going to test you on the lyrics. You have to say the lyrics of a song exactly. If you make a mistake, I get to give you a makeover."

I considered the idea. I could do it, easy-peasy. I'd probably win every time, but what would I do to her if she lost? While I was trying to figure that out, she said, "We'll call it the Lyrics Game."

"Okay. Cool. The Lola Bay Lyrics Game."

"Perfect. But I get to pick the song so you don't pick something so easy that you're sure to win. That's fair, right?"

That seemed fair. I knew them all. "Okay. Go ahead."

Dana walked around the room doing her hand thing, trailing her fingertips over things like she was going to pick up something. She turned her head left and right as if she was thinking really hard about which song would be hardest. A knot started twisting in my stomach. Which song would it be? My confidence began to fade.

She spun and pointed at me with a white-tipped fingernail. "'Thin Silver Wire.'"

I gulped. Okay. I could do that. It wasn't my favorite-favorite. But I knew it. "Okay."

"Wait," she said. "Let me have your phone."

"Why?"

"So I can pull up the lyrics, dude, and check you on them."

I handed over my phone. She tap, tap, tapped, and looked up. "Go."

I took a deep breath.

You try and tie your thin silver wire
around my heart but I rule me, not you.
You try and weave your thin silver wire
through my mind but I judge me, not you.
I'll leave you and snip that wire,
I'll bend it and snap it.
It's pretty but it hurts me, so take your
tightrope—

"Stop. Stop!!" yelled Dana.

"What?"

"You made a mistake!"

"I did not!"

"Yes you did. Look. You said, 'It's pretty but it hurts

me,' and there's no *it*. She says, 'It's pretty but hurts me.'"
She passed the phone back to me.

My shoulders sank—she was right. I couldn't believe I'd done that.

Dana made a smug face. "Hmm. I guess you have to let me give you a makeover."

Uh-oh. The possible seriousness of this began to register on me. Would she make me cut my bangs? Dread was rising. I looked at my phone again. It was 4:15. I thought about saying I had to go home.

Dana walked around me, studying me like she was trying to decide my fate.

I bit my lip. "Okay. Just tell me already."

She stared into my eyes. Her wavy hair in its place. Her short bangs all straight-straight. Her smile was diabolical. "Stand in front of the mirror."

She opened her closet door to reveal a full-length mirror. I stood up straight and squared my shoulders.

Dana examined my reflection—my hair, my T-shirt, my jeans, my tennis shoes. Then she picked up my hand and looked at it. "You have to let me give you a French manicure, and then you have to wear this." She pulled a flowered dress, a red sweater, and ankle boots out of her closet. "First, put these on."

"Wait." I know I agreed to be made over, but I didn't want to be dressed up to look like her. It wasn't me. Nope,

I didn't want to put on that flowered dress or those boots. If I did that, I'd be just like Melanie Fish Face's Imitators. "I can't wear the dress or the boots, but I'll put on the sweater. Okay?"

Dana looked at me and tipped her head. I think she was considering what would happen if she pushed me, and she guessed right. "Okay, just the sweater, but you have to let me give you a French manicure."

A puff of air escaped my lips. "Sure! Okay! Yeah!"

"Your nails are a nightmare."

I looked at them. They were kind of a nightmare by the standards of someone who was going to be a hand model when they grew up.

"So, sit over there." She pointed to her desk.

"Now?"

"Now. I'll be right back."

I sat at her desk and spread my hands out flat. My nails were short and stubby. When was the last time I'd clipped them or filed them? I couldn't remember, because my method was bite and chew. That might be coming to an end. An urge to stuff them in my pockets came over me. I distracted myself by snooping around the desk. There were piles of Lola Bay stuff, art books, and computer magazines, but no computer.

"Here we go." Dana walked in with a tray. On it was a bowl of warm soapy water, towels, bottles, cotton balls, and various implements. She set the tray down and reached to turn the music back on.

"Do not put on 'Thin Silver Wire,'" I said.

She laughed. "Deal. I bet you won't make that mistake again."

"Just wait until I pick your song."

"Oh, did I say I'd do it too?"

"Oh, you rat!"

"Shut up. I'll do it. Now stick your disgusting fingers in this bowl of soap."

It took a ridiculously long time for the polish to dry, and I had to be really careful answering the phone to tell Mom that I was on my way, but my nails looked totally beautiful. I held them up and waved them around.

"Don't wreck them!" Dana put my phone in my pocket and my backpack on my shoulders and pushed me out the door.

As I walked home, I waved my hands in the breeze to be extra sure they were dry, and I considered my new status as Dana's best friend. I wondered what Leeza would think if she knew, and I kind of hoped that she'd be jealous. I started to feel guilty, but then I guessed she was already best friends with Regina.

That night I had little appetite for dinner.

"Is anything the matter, Iris?" Mom asked.

I didn't want to say *I have a new best friend* because

it was so new that it felt like a secret, sort of like the staples in the baby pictures, and the mint tea, and the Lorna Doones were a secret, so I said, "No. Nothing."

"Where did you get that red sweater?" she asked.

"Oh, it's Dana's."

"Did she give it to you?"

"No. I'm just wearing it today. I got a makeover."

"A makeover?" she asked.

"Yeah, I lost the Lola Bay Lyrics Game." I held up my French manicure.

"Oh, nice," she said.

Then Ian and Echo started singing, "'The wheels on the bus go round and round,'" and I sang along.

7

MATCHING FRENCH MANICURES

THE NEXT MORNING when Leeza slammed into our seat on the bus, I already had my backpack positioned on my lap. Her eyes were on her phone as she robotically said, "Rah," but I slowly traced my French-manicured forefinger along the zipper so she couldn't miss it.

"Whoa, I. What did you do to your nails?"

I stuck my tongue out at her.

She shrugged.

I looked at them. They looked better and better to me all the time. Even the twins liked them.

Leeza finally conceded, "They look good, rah."

"Thanks."

"I suppose Dana did them?"

"Uh-huh."

"Are you going to start wearing dresses and ankle boots now?"

"No."

"And get that cocker spaniel haircut?"

"Shut up."

"I was just asking. Anyway. I was going to see if you wanted to come to my practice today and maybe go for pizza with us after?"

"You were? I mean, are you?"

She shrugged. "Yeah. Sure. We're still best friends, aren't we? Want to?"

Oh my gosh. Now what was I supposed to do? Leeza thought we were still best friends? Really? What about Regina? What about Dana? I was so confused.

Then Leeza said, "I mean, Dana can come too. If you want."

Something in me couldn't resist the invitation. It was like old times. "Okay. Sure, I'll come, and I'll ask her."

When we got off the bus, Leeza disappeared into the crush of kids. It didn't take long for me to find Dana. She was waiting for me at my locker.

"Let me see them."

I held out my fingers.

"Now be careful. You can't just slam your hands

around, you know. They're pretty tough but not inde-structible." She looked so happy.

"Yeah, I'm getting used to them."

"Where's the red sweater?"

"At home."

"You were supposed to wear it."

"I'm not wearing that every day or anything. It's still yours."

Kids shoved by us.

I was a little nervous about asking her to go to the volleyball practice. "So . . ."

"So? So do you want to play the Lola Bay Lyrics Game after school and you can give me a song?"

"Yeah, and if you lose, I can make you wear your red sweater!"

We laughed.

"But, I was thinking, maybe if you want to, you could go with me to Leeza's volleyball practice and then go for pizza after?"

Her face changed in an instant from happy to icky, like she'd eaten a bug. "You're going to Leeza's volleyball practice? I didn't know you did that."

"I don't. I mean, I haven't." I felt like I was apologiz-ing. "She just asked me, and I said I would, and she asked you too, so I thought we could, and I said I'd ask you. So don't you want to? And we could go for pizza?"

Her face went from icky to stony. "No, thanks, Iris. You go have fun with Leeza. I have other things to do." And she walked away.

✦ ✦ ✦

I was miserable the rest of the morning. Mom was happy. I'd called her to tell her about going to Leeza's practice.

"Do you need my credit card?"

"No. I can afford a piece of pizza. Thank you."

"Have fun."

"It's just a volleyball practice."

"I know. Have fun."

Groan.

In Studio Arts, I started a painting in the style of my influencers, manga artists. Dana stayed tucked behind her easel. With my first rounding brushstroke, Ms. Wells appeared over my shoulder and startled me.

"Hang on a second, Iris."

I paused my brush, blobbing paint in the middle of a smooth arc.

"How about something other than manga today? Something other than Lola Bay?"

I must have looked at her like I didn't understand.

"Come on, Iris. You're a creative. I know you have something else in you."

I was grateful for Ms. Wells having said I was a creative, and I didn't want to disappoint her, but honestly, my brain didn't have anything else in it.

"Just stop and close your eyes. Let your thoughts drift. They'll find something that attracts you."

I looked around. Some kids were working intently. Some were goofing around. None were looking at me. "You mean close my eyes right now?"

"Yes. Right now. Just for a couple minutes. Shut out the world."

Then she walked away. Leaving me with a wet paintbrush and an order to close my eyes in a room full of middle school kids. I turned my easel so the fewest people could see me and leaned over with my elbows on my knees and my chin in my hands. It felt pretty awkward and ridiculous. I sneaked one more glance in Dana's direction. She wasn't looking at me. I closed my eyes.

Tra la. First thing. Noise. I heard all the sounds of the room. Heat blowing out of the vent. Kids talking low. A stool creaking. Ms. Wells's voice in the distance. Brush-strokes scratching nearby. My own breathing. I got an itch on my cheek. I scratched it. I was thirsty. Forget about that. *Think about art things. Smells. Paint. Body odor. Lunch leftovers. Think about art things.*

The twins. Echo handing me one sticky piece of macaroni.

I shook my head to clear it.

Leeza on the bus with her head in her phone. Leeza playing volleyball.

I shook my head to clear it.

Eating oatmeal for breakfast. Walking to the bus. The brown-and-gray gardens. The brilliant bittersweet in Mr. Reynolds's front yard. Their dark vines and golden pods and orangey-red berries.

I snapped my eyes open. That was it. Bittersweet. I dipped the tip of my brush into dark umber and turned my arc into a vine. For the rest of the hour I was down the rabbit hole of painting something natural. Something without conflict. Except maybe that it was crowding out Mr. Reynolds's sumac bushes.

Ms. Wells came by and smiled. "You know, Iris, artists put pieces of themselves into their creations."

I looked at the bittersweet. I couldn't see any part of myself in it except that it grew on my block between Leeza's and my house. "Okay, Ms. Wells. Whatever you say." I looked at her like she was a little strange.

She laughed.

✦✦✦

When school was over, I walked up to the gym door alone. Muffled sounds of yelling, whistles, hip-hop music, and bouncing balls echoed into the hall. Goose bumps rose on my arm as I reached for the handle. When I pulled the door open, I was hit with ear-busting noise and the smell of sweat.

I was pretty sure the bleachers would be empty and I was almost right. On my side of the gym they were bare. On the other side, three seventh-grade boys sat in a group. Pimply Ted Eckles was in the middle, with a boy on either side of him. The bright lights and pounding warm-up music made me feel small as I scrambled up to the third level but stayed near the door.

"Hey, IRIS!"

Leeza was on the court waving at me, smiling.

"Hey, Leez!" I made a wide arc with my whole arm, then jammed my hands into my pockets. For two hours I watched the coach run the team through drills, divide them up into teams and play practice games, then run drills again. I was surprised how athletic Leeza looked. She seemed taller, leaner, and stronger. I realized her hair was shorter. How had I not noticed that before? I wondered when she'd gotten it cut. It wasn't that much shorter, maybe two inches, but she never would have cut it up to her shoulders like that before without consulting me.

Leeza's eyes were mostly on the coach or Ted Eckles. Once she caught my eye and tipped her head over to Ted, as if to say, *Look who's here.* I gave her a thumbs-up even though I didn't get it.

Not only was she stronger, but she played risky. She served wild balls. She dove under hard smash downs and slammed a few herself. Mostly she looked like she was having tons of fun. She was not the old Leeza who separated her M&M's into colors before she ate them.

And Regina. I didn't know she was such a good player. Turns out she was the captain of the team. Regina's hair was shoulder length, like Leeza's. Or maybe Leeza's was shoulder length like Regina's.

By the end of practice, my ears were ringing, and I felt like I'd been on display to the boys across the gym, who I'm sure were talking about me—like I was that fan-geek. I wished this was over. I wondered what Dana was doing. Probably sitting in her room hating me for being a jerk after being her best friend for only twenty-four hours. I wondered if this counted as betrayal.

The whistle blew and the team crowded around the coach. When they broke up, Leeza ran over to me. "Are you ready?"

Regina ran over. "Rah, Iris. You coming?"

I didn't know she knew my name. We'd never said one word to each other before. And here she was the captain of the volleyball team and Leeza's new friend and asking me if I was coming for pizza, and—this shocked me—using Leeza's *rah*. It felt a little like she was claiming Leeza as hers now.

"Come on, Iris. We gotta go." Leeza bumped into Regina and Regina bumped her back.

"Okay."

As I stood up, Leeza and Regina ran to the locker room. I didn't know what to do. Should I run after them or wait here? Then I saw the boys walking out.

"Hey, Iris," Ted called. He waved at me to follow them.

I took a deep breath. Oh boy. I'd thought it would just be me and Leeza and maybe some girls from the team. I'd never guessed the boys would be going along. I looked more closely at the other two. One was Ray Krishnamurti. He'd always been decent to me. I mean, like he never called me a name or made an ugly face at me like some boys did to some girls. I knew he ran track. The other one was Robert Benally. He was quiet like Ted. I didn't think I'd ever heard him say a word in school that he wasn't forced to say. He was in Studio Arts and drew birds on everything—his artwork, his notebooks, his book covers. And not just any birds. Beautiful birds of many kinds, each with sharp blue eyes.

We stood around the locker room entrance until Leeza and Regina burst out.

"Let's haul." Regina led the pack.

I still didn't exactly know where we were going or

how we were getting there. Leeza threw her arm around me and pulled me along.

"I'm so glad you're here."

I nodded. "Where're we going?"

"Pizza Papa's. It's just around the corner."

I'd never been to Pizza Papa's before. It had a rickety old door, a half-lit beer sign in the window, and long tables with red-and-white-checked tablecloths.

"Don't worry. It's not a bar." Leeza had read my mind. "My folks have approved this place. The owner knows my dad. His name is Peter. Peter Papa!" Leeza laughed.

I ordered a cheese slice and water. Leeza got veggie. Regina got the house special. The boys each ordered three slices.

"Good practice, Leeza," Regina said, and toasted her with her bottle of water. "You could be co-captain."

"I didn't know you could play like that," I said.

Leeza looked hurt.

"I don't mean I didn't think you could. I just didn't know you *did*, I mean," I apologized.

Leeza laughed. "That's what practice will do, I guess."

We sat in awkward silence. I tried not to look directly at the particularly giant pimple on the end of Ted's nose. It wasn't his fault. I supposed it could happen to any of us. I sure hoped one wouldn't sprout on my face. Ray drummed his fingers. Regina bumped shoulders with

Leeza. Robert studied the can of Coke in front of him.

"Alfred got out last night and we spent all night looking for him," said Ted.

Leeza and Regina gasped. I wasn't sure how shocked to be, not knowing who Alfred was. His little brother, maybe?

Robert spoke. "Don't you lock the cage?"

"Naw. Not like with a padlock or anything. It's got a latch. Benny just didn't close it good enough. Dude, it was funny."

"Oh yeah? Where'd you find him?" asked Ray.

"It was so crazy. My sister started screaming and we thought she was going to smash Alfred over the head. Then Benny started crying, and my mom started yelling, and my sister kept screaming. Alfred was in her closet."

"Is Alfred okay?" asked Leeza.

"Oh yeah. He's fine. It was really, really funny. He almost met his doom with a tennis racket."

Just then the pizza arrived. The slices were as big as half of a regular pizza. Mine hung over the plate with its cheese sizzling and dripping on the table.

The boys' plates were oozing cheese and pepperoni and hamburger. They dug in and washed them down with milk, water, and Cokes. Somewhere in the middle of the feast, I asked, "What is Alfred?"

"He's a bearded dragon," said Ted through a mouthful of pizza.

"How big is he?" I asked.

"About two feet long."

"Whoa. That's no small lizard. No wonder your sister was screaming," I said.

"I have a dog, like a normal person," said Robert.

"Me too," said Regina.

Leeza looked at me, and we both busted out laughing. We knew she had probably forty-five pets of all sizes, shapes, and species at her house. Then we said out loud at the same time, "But no lizards."

"What?" said Ted.

"What are you talking about?" asked Regina.

"Oh, nothing," I said.

"Yeah, nothing," said Leeza.

It felt good to have that little private joke with Leeza.

Regina licked her fingers and wiped her mouth, then asked, "So, Iris, are you thinking about playing volleyball?"

Before I could answer, Leeza guffawed. I thought she was going to choke on her Coke. "No way! Iris would never play sports."

"Correct. I might be the best volleyball player in the world, but we'll never know it because I'll never try."

"Why not?" asked Regina.

"Not my thing."

"Iris is an artist, not a jock," said Robert.

"Like you, Robert," said Ray with a trill in his voice. "Woooo."

Robert rolled his eyes and shrugged. "Just saying. Not everybody plays sports. Some of us are *arteests*."

I watched all of this happening like it was going on in slow motion, wondering what Dana would think of it if she were there.

Ted slammed his shoulder into Robert's. Robert threatened to pour his milk on Ted. Everyone laughed except me. I thought about Robert the bird boy saying I was an *arteest*. It was kind of cool that another artist thought I could paint. I searched my brain for something to say to Robert about art.

Before I could think of anything, he said, "Those branches with the orange balls were really nice."

"Uh, thanks" was all I could think of to say, because at the same exact moment, Melanie Fish Face and the Imitators crowded through the door of Pizza Papa's and took over an entire corner. They were so into themselves, they didn't notice us. Or at least they didn't notice me. The last thing I needed was Fish Face coming over and hassling me in front of all these kids, but then

I thought, *No, she wouldn't tangle with Regina and Leeza,* and I relaxed.

I relaxed, that is, until Leeza said something to Regina, and Regina slammed the table with her fist, and they both busted out snort-laughing. It occurred to me that I might not want to tangle with them either.

NOSY MOTHERS

MOM WAS WAY too happy when I got home.

She hummed as she steered the twins upstairs to get ready for bed. "How was the practice and pizza with Leeza? What a nice afternoon!"

"Relax. It was fine. That's all."

She turned Echo over to me with a questioning look on her face.

"Come on, Echo. Race you to your room!" I said.

"Fingers," Echo demanded, meaning she wanted to see my French manicure again.

"Where did you go for pizza?" Mom called from the bathroom.

"Pizza Papa's," I yelled back as I wrestled Echo into her pajamas.

"Right, that's what Leeza's mom said. Was it good?"

"Then why did you ask me? Yes, it was fine. The pizza slices were huge."

"Honestly, Iris. I'm just happy for you that you and Leeza spent some time together again." She scooted Ian into the bedroom. "I heard there were other kids along. I don't know the Krishnamurtis or the Benallys."

"Ugh! Why do you have to know every middle school parent?" I wasn't sure why this was irritating every last one of my nerves, but it was.

"Because I'm your mother."

"I think maybe you just like Leeza better than Dana, that's all. They're my friends. It's my choice."

Mom moved the bedtime books to the floor and sat down. Ian crawled into her lap. "I never said I didn't like Dana. Where did that come from?"

My anger rose. "You asked her a gazillion questions."

"READ!" cried Echo.

"Hold on a minute." Now Mom was upset.

"READ!" cried Echo, poking me with her book.

"I never once said I didn't like Dana," she said. "I don't know her. She comes and goes without being very sociable, that's all." Mom opened a book, then shut it again.

"I have a right to know if she's a nice girl. That's my job as a mom."

"A nice girl? So, Mom, is Dana a nice girl? You must think so because you still let her come here."

"I can't say that I know her. You're different with her."

"She's a year older than me, Mom. I'm older now too. I'm a sixth grader now. I'm not a little kid."

Mom studied my angry red face. "You tell me, Iris. Is Dana a nice girl? Is she polite? Is she kind? Does she have good values? Is she worthy of your friendship?"

"READ!" cried Echo.

Mom opened the book again, and Ian started turning the pages himself and making up the story.

I could feel my temper about to blow. I thought we were talking about why Mom had to know all the parents of everyone I was friends with, but now I was being asked to prove Dana was worthy of me.

A blur of scenes flickered through my mind: Dana standing up for me against Melanie Fish Face, all the fun we had fangirling Lola Bay, Melanie Fish Face blaming her for stapling the baby face, her mom not sticking up for her, her dad being willing to throw a can of paint on someone for her, her making me her best friend and having a secret snack and a game. But there was hacking the library and trying to get free Lola Bay merch and her being mad at me for going to the volleyball practice.

"She's nice to me." I didn't say *Not everyone has been kind to her*, because I knew that would set off alarm bells for Mom. "Are you wondering if I'm a nice girl now?"

Mom's eyes flashed. "Don't do that, Iris."

"What? You are ruining this whole day."

"Did something happen with Leeza today?"

"What are you talking about? No!" I heard the garage door go up. Dad was home. I felt a rush of relief. He would come up and make corny jokes and put an end to this awful conversation.

But Mom pressed. "Iris. Did something happen with Leeza today? Or Regina? Or one of those boys? You are clearly upset about something."

"No. No. No. No. NO. Nothing happened. Leeza plays volleyball now, and she's really good. And she likes Ted, and she's friends with Regina. Robert liked my branches and orange balls. That's all. Okay?"

Mom's eyebrows almost flew off her forehead. "What do you mean, he likes your branches and orange balls?"

I gave her my most exasperated look. "I painted bittersweet in Studio Arts, Mom! Robert paints birds. That's all."

"Calm down, honey. I understand now. Branches and orange balls."

Dad's voice boomed into the room. "What's this about branches and orange balls? Did you know Apollo's crown was made of bay leaves?"

I must have had trouble written on my face, because Dad looked from me to Mom and back again, and said, "What's wrong?"

Mom stared at me and waited for my response.

"Nothing. No one understands how hard my life is!" I reached for Echo. "Come here. I'll read to you." And I read Echo her book. And another. And another.

✦ ✦ ✦

I soaked my pillow with tears and soothed myself with Lola Bay's *Celery Bouquet* album over and over. I especially connected with "Why Can't You Be Like Me?" I needed everyone to be like me for just a day.

When I opened my eyes, I still had my clothes on. I thought it was the middle of the night, but the clock said 6:28 a.m. My room was dark and my eyes burned. I'd told Dad to go away last night and he had. Neither Mom nor Dad had come back to bother me. I wasn't sure how I felt about that. Couldn't they see how upset I was? What kind of parents were they, anyway?

I had to go find Dana as soon as I got to school. I needed to make her not mad at me and tell her the volleyball practice was not that much fun and she wouldn't have wanted to go to the pizza place because Melanie Fish Face was there.

When I got downstairs, Dad was in the kitchen eating cereal.

"You're up early," he said.

I slunk into a chair. "Yeah."

"Are you hungry?"

"A little."

He pushed the Fruity O's box toward me and got up and grabbed a bowl, a spoon, and the milk. "Did you get any sleep?"

I nodded.

Pink and yellow O's cascaded into the plastic bowl, followed by a gush of milk and the scrape of the spoon. The milk was cold in my stomach. After a few scoops, I said, "Sorry."

Dad chewed. "I get it. Sometimes things are tough."

"You do?"

"Sure. I was in sixth grade once."

I almost spit my cereal across the table. Dad in sixth grade! That must have been hilarious. "It's different now in the new world."

He laughed. "Right. It was the old days. But kids were still trying to figure out friendships."

I gave him a side look. "You know about friendships?"

"A little."

"But not girls."

"No. Not girls," he admitted.

I sighed. "I didn't think so."

"But, you know, Mom does. She was a girl."

My shoulders tensed. "Oh no."

"Okay. Okay. All in good time. But you know we love you, and we're here for you, and we want you to be safe both physically and emotionally."

I wasn't hungry anymore. The twins were making noise upstairs and they would be down with Mom any minute. "I know."

"Do you want a ride to school?"

"Sure."

Dana avoided me for most of the morning. I'd see her coming down the hall and not know what to do. Should I wave or say hi? Wait for her or turn away? She made the decision for us and slipped in other directions. It was like one little hurt after another until I resolved we were not going to be friends anymore and all because I went to Leeza's volleyball practice.

Then right before lunch, I turned a corner and she was waiting for me with her arms folded.

"Well?" she asked as if I was supposed to say something.

"Well . . ." I said. I thought I was ready to talk about yesterday, but I couldn't figure out what to say.

"Well," she said. "I accept your apology. Don't ever do that to me again. Okay? Good."

Before I could think it through, I said, "Good."

It happened so fast. She skipped right over my having to say anything. I wasn't planning to apologize. I mean, I wanted to explain and say sorry she felt hurt.

It was as if a switch flipped. She nodded and almost smiled. "See? I'm giving you a second chance."

She was giving me a second chance?

"I hope you know that Leeza only asked you to come to her practice because she is jealous that you and I are best friends now."

"Do you think so?"

"Of course. I can tell. I'm older. Did you tell her we are best friends?"

I thought about when Leeza and I were on the bus and she saw my manicure and she asked me to come to the practice and she said she and I were still best friends. It all seemed so obvious. "Oh my gosh, I think you're right. She saw my manicure. She was jealous."

"You really shouldn't talk to her anymore."

"Not talk to Leeza?"

"That's the best thing."

"I don't know."

"Trust me. A person cannot have two best friends. And she's not your best friend anymore anyway, right?"

Just then, the bell rang.

"I'll see you in Studio Arts," she said, and waved. "After school you can give me a Lola Bay Lyrics Game song. Make it super-hard. I will pass, I'm sure!"

I walked in a daze. Did being best friends with Dana really mean I couldn't talk to Leeza anymore? How would that even be possible? She had been my best friend since forever. Suddenly, I became terrified of seeing Leeza in the cafeteria.

Halfway through the food line, with an apple and plain spaghetti on my tray, I considered tossing it into the garbage and not eating. Then I looked around, and Leeza was sitting with Regina. I don't know why I was worried I'd run into her. That's where she'd been eating most days lately. The first day it happened I felt stabbed in the heart. Today I was relieved. I steered to the table with Salima and Callie.

"Hi. Where're Bethany and Paige?" I asked.

"They're not here yet," said Callie. "Where's Leeza?"

"She's over there with Regina." I looked again and realized Ted was at the table too. "And Ted."

"Ooooh, Ted!" Salima and Callie said at the same time. "Leeza and Ted."

I sat down. "Yeah."

I looked at my plate of spaghetti. It looked sad. All white and limp and uncovered. I picked up one strand with my fingertips.

"WOW, you got a French manicure," Callie squealed. "It's so nice."

"Did Dana do that for you?"

"Yeah. We played the Lola Bay Lyrics Game and I lost, and that's what she got to do. Give me a manicure."

Callie and Salima became immediately interested in the Lola Bay Lyrics Game, so I explained it to them. By the time I was done, some of my sadness had lifted and they asked if they could play. Then I got this great idea that the Unofficial Lola Bay Fan Club could have more members, and meet and do things like play the Lyrics Game and even more fun things.

"You know we have the Unofficial Lola Bay Fan Club now. I'm the president. Melanie Fisher and her friends aren't in it. They aren't allowed. It's so much more fun. If you want to join, I can get you membership cards."

"We do!" said Salima. "Will we get French manicures?"

"I have to talk to Dana about that. She's the French manicure expert. I'll let you know."

Bethany and Paige arrived at the table.

"What about French manicures?" asked Bethany, who loved a good manicure.

"Look at Iris's fingers," said Salima.

I fanned my hands.

"Nice," said Bethany. "Dana do that?"

"Uh-huh."

"If you win—wait, or lose, I'm not sure which—the Lola Bay Lyrics Game, you can get a manicure like that," said Salima.

"Wait, no, not exactly," I said.

"How do I play?" asked Bethany. "I'm in."

This was getting out of control. "Just wait. I have to talk to Dana. We'll let you know when the next meeting of the Unofficial Lola Bay Fan Club is."

Bethany and Paige sat down, and I got the heck out of there. This was too complicated. I had no idea what Dana would think about it. And that reminded me that Leeza was a member of the Unofficial Lola Bay Fan Club and I wasn't supposed to talk to her anymore. My stomach twinged a little bit.

✦ ✧ ✦

In Studio Arts, Dana stopped by my easel. "Hey."

I was using markers to draw my signature manga version of Lola Bay with the deep-set purple eyes. "Hey. Guess what?"

Her eyebrows arched. "What?"

"There are some kids who want to join the Unofficial Lola Bay Fan Club."

Her eyes switched to a squint. "Really? Who?"

"Callie, Salima, Bethany, and Paige."

She looked shocked. "Really?"

"They asked me about my manicure and I told them about the Lola Bay Lyrics Game and the club, and they wanted to join and play."

Dana rolled her eyes. "And you just invited them in? You are such a sixth grader sometimes."

That was way harsh. I thought I was more mature all the time.

My voice may have been a little feeble, but I said it. "They just want to join our club and be like us."

Dana's eyes flashed. "Like *us*?"

AN OFFICIAL MEETING OF THE UNOFFICIAL LOLA BAY FAN CLUB

SATURDAY AFTERNOON WE had our first big group meeting of the Unofficial Lola Bay Fan Club. Dana had come around to the idea that it might be good to be bigger than Melanie Fish Face's Lola Bay Fan Club.

I put away all the toys in our family room, wiped the toddler sticky stuff off everything, and vacuumed up the crumbs. Mom was so overly excited about it that she made brownies, and a fruit plate, and punch, and took the twins to the park. Dad worked in his office upstairs and promised to stay out of the way.

Dana patched three of my fingernails because they had gotten dinged during the week.

"You have to learn to be more careful with these."

"I know. I know. I'm trying."

We'd worked a long time on rules for the game. It was a lot harder than when we first made it up. Dana typed them on my computer and printed them out. The membership cards were ready. We'd voted her vice president so there weren't any open offices. And it was her idea to have the meeting while Leeza had a volleyball game so there wouldn't be any awkward decisions for her about coming. I didn't think she would come even if she didn't have a game. The only way Leeza was coming to a Lola Bay meeting anymore was if Ted Eckles was there. Or Regina.

At 2:00 p.m. we put on Lola Bay music and waited. We were wearing our black tees and all the bracelets we had between us. Within minutes, the doorbell rang and all four of them came in together. I was so happy to see they had on black tees and bracelets too. They huddled together and moved to the family room like a small flock of flamingos.

They lined up next to each other on the couch.

Dana waved at me to start talking.

"Welcome to the Unofficial Lola Bay Fan Club. We are happy you are here. It's so much fun. And way better than the other one. Especially since we have the Lola Bay Lyrics Game."

They all clapped, which gave me a thrill.

"So we have snacks over there for after the game. But

you could eat some now if you want. My mom said to tell you that the punch has pineapple juice in case anyone is allergic. She cut up the fruit in shapes, which is kind of cheesy—but sort of cute. Now, Dana is going to explain the game."

Dana stood up. Her nails had just been done, so she held the paper with the rules like it was from a museum. It showed off her hands.

"Welcome. I'm the vice president of the Unofficial Lola Bay Fan Club of Minnesota. As you know, Iris is the president. And we have so many more things to offer than the other group. Mostly we are super-inclusive. We make up our own activities. We have crafts. And we have the one and only Lola Bay Lyrics Game."

She patted her hair before continuing. "Iris is going to hand out the rules, and I am going to go over them with you."

I passed out the pages to each of them.

Dana read from the pages:

THE LOLA BAY LYRICS GAME
★ ☆ ★

Who can play: Any official member of the Unofficial
Lola Bay Fan Club

What is a turn: A turn is when one member names
a Lola Bay song for another member and that

member has to say the words to that song
perfectly. If they don't, then the person who
made the mistake has to let the other person
give them a makeover.

EXAMPLE: Dana named a song for Iris. Iris missed
a word. Dana gave Iris a manicure because her
nails were so gross.

Things you can't do to someone: Anything dangerous.
Anything unhealthy. Anything illegal.

Dana looked up from reading. "Everyone understand?"

Bethany said, "So are you giving us French manicures today?"

She said, "Well, not me. If you lose, you may get one, but not from me."

"What about pedicures?" asked Paige.

"It's not only about manicures and pedicures," said Dana, who was getting irritated.

"What if I lose to you?" asked Bethany.

"You won't. I'll be Iris's partner."

"How do you pick partners?" asked Salima.

"You just agree," I said. "I guess if you can't agree, we could draw names."

"I'll be partners with Callie," said Salima.

"I'll be partners with Paige," said Bethany.

"Good. That works great," said Dana.

I started wondering if this was such a good idea. Everyone was obsessed with getting a French manicure, and I suppose anyone could give one, but everyone except Dana would probably be horrible at it.

"Okay, which team wants to go first?" Dana asked.

Callie raised her hand. "We'll go!"

"Who's going to name the song?" asked Dana.

"I'll name the song," said Callie. "I pick 'Waveless Sea.'"

"Hang on." Dana grabbed my phone and pulled up the lyrics. "Ready? Start, Salima."

Salima stood up straight and closed her eyes like she was concentrating really hard.

Soaring on wings above a waveless sea.
See me. See me.
Wake up from your rhythmless sleep.
See me. See me.
Where are you—

"STOP. STOP!" yelled Dana.

Salima's eyelids flew open. "What?"

"It's 'where were you,' not 'where are you.' Sorry, Salima, you lose." Dana pointed to her partner. "Callie?"

Callie looked excited.

Salima said, "Am I going to get a French manicure?"

"Oh my gosh, dudes," I said. "Stop with the manicures. It's anything!"

"Pick anything," said Dana.

"Like what?" asked Callie. "Should I dare her to do a cartwheel?"

"It's not Truth or Dare!" said Dana. "You do a makeover thing."

"Okay, Salima, let me fix your hair," said Callie.

Salima shrugged. "Sure. Okay."

Callie looked around and her eyes rested on the twins' toy box. She went digging and came up with a pail of watercolor markers. For the next ten minutes she colored the tips of Salima's hair in neon pink, blue, and green. We all clapped and marveled at how cool it looked on Salima's chestnut brown hair. She went into the bathroom to look.

"What do you think?" Callie called. "I think Lola Bay would love it. She might even do hers that way."

Salima didn't sound so sure. "It's okay. I don't think my mom is going to like it."

"She'll get over it," said Dana. "Besides, it's just watercolor. It washes out. Who's next?"

"We are," said Bethany. "I'll pick a song for Paige."

"Okay. What's the song?" asked Dana.

"I pick 'Reflections,'" said Bethany.

Paige looked nervous.

Dana scrolled for the lyrics and, when she had them, said, "Okay, Paige, go."

Paige rolled her eyes.

Do you remember what you said?
What you did?
Do you remember what I didn't do?
I've had some time to think about it
And here's what I have to say to you.

"STOP. STOP!" called Dana.

Paige looked surprised.

I was surprised too. I thought she'd said it perfectly.

Dana looked fake sorry for Paige. "There's no *and* before 'Here's what I have to say to you.'"

Paige reached for the phone in disbelief. "Let me see."

Her face fell and she turned to Bethany. "Okay. What are you going to do to me? Do something good."

Bethany jumped up and looked around. "Iris, do you have any makeup?"

"I have lip gloss."

"I mean real makeup, like eye makeup."

"No. I don't have that."

"Does your mom?"

My mind jumped to the bathroom in my parents' bedroom and the drawer with only lipstick and mascara. Such a sad amount of makeup. "No."

Bethany started rummaging through the twins' toy box.

"No way are you putting marker on my eyelids," said Paige.

Bethany popped up with a box of watercolors and two tubes of glitter glue. "Perfect!"

Paige grabbed for the glitter glue, and Bethany held it away. She read the label out loud. "Water soluble. See? It's perfectly safe. Now sit down. I'll do watercolor on your eyelids and a glitter rainbow under your brows."

Paige slumped into a chair with a distrustful expression. "This better look good!"

"You'll be beautiful," said Bethany.

We all crowded around and watched Bethany paint pink on Paige's eyelids and squeeze lines of glitter glue above it. Lime green, then bright blue, then pink. She used the tip of the tube to blend the edges. Then she fanned it with a magazine until it dried.

"Now don't move your eyelids," said Bethany, "or you'll ruin it."

"I *can't* hardly move my eyelids," said Paige. "They won't go up. They only open halfway, and they crackle."

"Try and blink," I told her.

"I can't." Paige started waving her hands and bouncing in her chair. "Help!"

Dana pressed her hand on her shoulder. "Stop it, Paige. It's no big deal."

"Don't be a baby. You have to look at it," said Bethany, and she pulled Paige to the bathroom.

We all crowded in and watched Paige tip her head left and right, up and down, as she tried to decide if she liked it. The longer we looked at it, the less it looked like a clown and the more it looked beautiful.

Finally, Paige pronounced, "It's not so bad. I like it okay, but I'm ready to take it off."

"Wait," said Bethany. "Let me take pictures first."

Bethany took pictures while Dana grabbed a washcloth off the towel bar and turned on the warm water. "I'll fill the sink with soapy water and we can blot it off."

"Oh, all my beautiful work," moaned Bethany.

"Should we wash off my hair?" Salima asked. "I don't think my mom will like it."

"Pictures first," said Bethany.

Dana squeezed the warm washcloth and laid it over Paige's eyes. "Just hold it there till it melts the glue."

At exactly that second, I heard the front door open and the twins hit the house. It was followed by "Iris?"

"Oh my gosh, my mom is home!"

"Where is everyone?" she called. "Did you try the brownies?"

"We're in the bathroom. We'll be right out."

"All of you? What are you doing in there?"

". . . Nothing."

The next instant Mom was trying to open the bathroom door, but of course she couldn't, because six of us were standing by the mirror next to it.

"What's going on in there, Iris?"

"Nothing!"

"Is someone sick?"

"No. Go away. We'll be out in a minute."

I turned to Paige and Dana to see how it was going, and uh-oh. The glue was melting, all right. It was melting, and streams of lime green, bright blue, and hot pink were running down Paige's face and dripping on the towel she was holding under her chin. Her eyes were closed tight and she started flapping her hands again and crying. "Ewwww."

"Cool," said Bethany. "You have rivers of glitter sliding down your cheeks."

Mom must have heard Paige because she turned the knob again, and this time some of us squished to the side. She had a clear view of what looked like Dana dabbing glitter *on* Paige's eyes.

"What in the world. Dana, what are you doing?"

"I'm fixing Paige's face."

"Help!" squeaked Paige.

"Move!" Mom pushed into the bathroom like a general and grabbed the washcloth and started barking, "What is it?"

"Watercolors and glitter glue," I answered.

"Go get the containers!"

We all fell over ourselves running to the family room to get the paint box and glitter tubes. Bethany grabbed them first because she knew where she had put them down, and handed them over. By this time Mom had managed to pat the glitter off Paige's eyelids and was working on her cheeks. It was coming off easily enough, but her skin was stained with rivulets of color. The rest of us looked at each other and backed away.

Mom read the backs of the containers and seemed to calm down. She kept draining and refilling the sink with clean, cool water. Soon, Paige was calm and the paint and glitter was almost all gone from her face, except for a few specks in her eyebrows. She only had a faint glow of green and blue around her eyes and the palest streak stains of pink on her cheeks.

We all went to the family room and Mom yelled, "Oh no!"

We looked, and the twins had gotten into the brownies and fruit and punch and what they hadn't eaten was being served to their stuffed animals.

"Okay, I think this meeting of the Unofficial Lola Bay Fan Club is over," said Mom.

We all knew it.

Then Salima said, "Do you think you can get this out of my hair, Mrs. Underwood?"

A strange quiet came over Mom. She looked at me and seemed to be about to speak, and then her gaze scanned the rest of us, and she said, "I will deal with Salima's hair while the rest of you clean this up. You, Iris, clean up the twins."

Mom and Salima went to the bathroom and shut the door.

Dana put on some Lola Bay and we started picking up and cleaning. We carried the dishes to the kitchen, and I washed up the twins at the kitchen sink.

When we were almost done, Dad came down with a big smile on his face. "Hi, girls. How's it going? Any brownies left for your old man?"

I answered through a clenched jaw. "No, the brownies are gone. Can you take the twins upstairs? Mom came home early and they got into everything. I cleaned them up." Then I took a deep breath and gave him a look.

He hoisted Echo onto his hip and reached for Ian's hand. "Where's Mom?"

"She's in the bathroom. I wouldn't go in there right now."

He didn't argue. He looked at each of us and noticed Paige's rainbow hue. His eyes flashed, but he remained expressionless. "Okay. Come on, kiddos. Let's go upstairs and read some books."

"Books!" said Echo.

"Brownies!" said Ian.

"No more brownies, buddy," said Dad.

As he hustled the twins upstairs, the hair dryer started blowing in the bathroom. I wished that Salima's hair color had washed out, just like I'd been wishing that Paige's face would go back to normal.

Dana, Callie, Bethany, Paige, and I sat in the family room. Paige kept asking if it was gone. We said it was getting fainter every minute. After about ten minutes the bathroom door opened and Salima came out.

We all cried, "Wow!"

Her hair looked really good. The marker color wasn't completely gone, but it was pale enough that you could only see it if the light hit it right.

"That's so cool!" said Callie. "You are welcome."

"I didn't say thank you," said Salima, "but it is kind of cool and it will probably be gone the next time I wash it."

Mom went straight to Paige with a tissue and a tube of aloe vera cream. "Let me put a little more of this on you, Paige," she said, gently wiping it on her eyelids and cheeks. Amazingly, most of the remaining color came off on the tissue. Mom closed her eyes and sighed. "There. That's nice."

Paige, Salima, Bethany, and Callie all stood up.

"We have to go," said Callie.

"Yeah, we'll see you in school," said Salima.

They walked to the door, once again a group.

I followed them. "Do you want to sign membership cards?" I asked.

They all poked and pushed each other, trying to get out.

"I'll think about it," said Salima.

"Me too," said Callie. "Maybe. But I'm not sure."

"I don't think so," said Paige.

"No, thanks," said Bethany.

And they were gone.

When I got back to the family room, Mom was perched rigidly on the edge of the sofa and Dana was standing with her arms folded like she had been that day in her driveway with her mom.

"I want you both to sit down," Mom said. "And turn off the music."

I quickly reached for my phone and turned it off. I wanted to start talking, but I waited.

Mom started. "I don't know what ever possessed you two to do this. It's a great disappointment. It could have been dangerous. Salima's hair is one thing, but Paige's eyes! What were you thinking? What this has to do with being a music fan club, I just don't know." She shook her head.

I reached for the rules of the game and tried to hand them to her, but she pushed them away.

"Iris, I'm speechless as to what to do about this right now. I'm not sure what you can say to me that will improve the situation. I know this, though. Neither one of you should tell me it wasn't your fault. I know you didn't put the marker on Salima's hair, but you let it happen. I know you didn't put the paint and glitter on Paige's face, but you let it happen."

Dana looked like she was struggling to say something, but she didn't, and I was glad. Because I was afraid they would get into an argument and she'd get banished from our house.

I had to deal with this. "We're sorry it went this way."

Mom looked at me, then at Dana, then back to me, and said, "Well, that's something."

10

THE SWORD OVER OUR HEADS

DANA GATHERED UP her things in my room.

"You never should have invited them to join the club."

"You said it was okay!"

"What was I supposed to do? You'd already done it. Now Melanie Fish Face is going to find out and tell the whole world."

This bugged me. "Stop caring about Melanie Fish Face so much! No one cares about her."

"You don't know that. You're a sixth grader. Seventh graders care. They'll think I tried to blind Paige."

"No, they won't. If anyone says anything, I'll tell them Bethany did it."

"Great. That will make you really popular."

"I don't care if I'm popular."

"Do you care if people think the Unofficial Lola Bay Fan Club is a joke? Because if they find out about the game going like it did today, they will. These things spread fast. It's probably all over the school by now."

I threw a pillow on the floor. "Of course I care!"

Dana picked it up and threw it back at me with force. "That's why we should keep the club to ourselves. Get it?"

I threw it back at her and screamed, "I GET IT."

She threw it back at me. "GOOD."

I flopped on my bed and hugged my pillow.

"I'm going home."

I didn't say anything, but I thought, *Good*.

I expected Mom to come up and talk to me after Dana left, but she didn't. Then I thought Dad would, but he didn't.

I overheard Mom on the phone talking to Salima's mother, explaining it was "water soluble" and would be "gone in the next wash." Next she called Paige's mother and said, "A little aloe vera should get rid of the rest of it." Her tone was light. I didn't hear her say *sorry*. She said things like, "Sometimes they are still little girls," and "Sometimes they don't always think things through." She wasn't exactly begging for forgiveness or blaming anyone either.

Then I thought they would bring up the whole mess at dinner and let loose on me . . . but they didn't.

I kept my ears perked to hear if my mom called Dana's, but . . . she didn't.

✦✧✦

After dinner, my curiosity about whether the news was really all over the school was out of control. Even though I wasn't supposed to talk to Leeza, I decided to go over and see if she'd heard anything.

I used to just barge right in, but I felt a little nervous, not having been there in a while, so I rang the bell. Her little brother Jacob yanked the door open, yelled, "IT'S IRIS," and ran. The Todd house was full of the usual bedlam. The TV was blasting, kids were running in circles, and someone was crying. I made my way to the kitchen, where I knew I'd find her mom.

Mrs. Todd was up to her elbows in purple water in the sink. "Hey there, Iris! How are you? We haven't seen you in a while."

Her voice calmed my jitters. This kitchen with its purple water was as much home as my own. "What are you doing?"

"I'm dyeing a set of sheets for Christine's Halloween costume. She's going to be a grape. Sit down."

"Is Leeza home?"

Four-year-old Christine, six-year-old Jacob, and eight-year-old Randall chased each other through the kitchen with wands, screaming. Just as I knew she would, Mrs. Todd ignored it. "No, the team is doing a Saturday night pizza party."

"Oh, okay." I got up.

The kids made another shrieking lap through the kitchen.

"Be careful running with those wands," Mrs. Todd yelled. "Iris, I miss seeing you around here." Then she laughed. "Don't suppose you miss this madhouse!"

I smiled. "It's good to see you all too."

"You come around more, you hear?"

"Uh-huh." I turned to leave.

"Iris, is everything okay?"

"Oh yeah. Everything's fine."

I left thinking I definitely wouldn't be in this house as much as before. Maybe never again. As I passed bikes, balls, and superhero capes strewn on the front lawn, I pulled my jacket tightly around me.

When I slipped back into the house through the back door, Mom was waiting.

"Are you ready to talk about this afternoon?" she asked.

"What?"

"I've given you some time to think about it, so sit down, let's talk."

The kitchen chair legs scraped as I pulled it out.

Mom's voice was calm and steady. "What do you have to say about the fan club today?"

That's when I realized I'd spent more time wondering why she wasn't yelling at me than thinking about what I would say when she did. Something told me to choose my words carefully.

"I never should have invited other girls to join the club. Then none of this would have happened."

Mom was folding and refolding a dish towel as she talked. "That's certainly one choice you could have made. But there's nothing wrong with having a bigger club. It's really about other choices, don't you think?"

"Like what? Like playing the Lola Bay Lyrics Game? Mom! We had good rules. Safe rules. Everyone knew them. It was Callie who put the markers on—"

She put her hand up. "Wait a second, Iris. Hold on. I read your rules. They were good. But when Callie pulled the markers out of the toy box and when Bethany un-capped the glitter glue, what did you think? Did you have any thoughts about whether those were good ideas?"

A giant defense started to well up in my chest. I almost rose off my chair. Then I thought back to the very moment when the glitter caps were coming off. Even though a small voice in the back of my mind had said this might be trouble, I was totally having fun. I didn't worry until Paige got upset.

"I suppose, a little."

"You suppose? A little? You're the one who told me you were growing up. If that's true, you have to start making choices like a more mature person, or you can't be in situations like these."

I strained to imagine what a more grown-up me should have done. "Mom, I couldn't stop them."

"Of course you could have stopped them. It's your house. And what about Dana? She's a year older. She should have known better. You know, Iris, the year between sixth and seventh grade makes a big difference in maturity. That may be the whole problem here."

What was she saying? Dana's being in seventh grade was why this all happened? Was she blaming Dana? My temper shot up. "I figured you would find a way to blame Dana."

"No. No. I'm not putting it all on her, but I'm saying she has a lot of influence over you, and I need to see you making better choices for yourself in your friendship with her."

"Oh my gosh. *I* invited them to the club. *I'm* the one who told them about the manicures and got them confused. *She's* the one who tried to get the glue off. *She's* the one who told me not to invite more kids. You are so unfair to her."

"Listen to me, Iris. Luckily, this turned out okay. But the Iris who started sixth grade is not the same Iris I'm looking at right now. I know things with Leeza are different and that's been hard, and I know Dana has been a new friend when you needed one. And I know middle school is a big change. But you have to make healthy and safe choices for yourself."

The tight hot feeling in my throat told me tears were coming. I felt my face getting red.

Mom's voice softened. "What do you want, Iris? What would make you happiest right now?"

So much. I wanted so much. Or maybe not all that much. Did I want Leeza to be the old Leeza? No, not exactly. Did I want Dana to be any different? No, not really. Did I wish we hadn't had the meeting? Oh yeah, for sure. But what did I really want?

"I want to be left alone to fangirl Lola Bay and have the club with Dana. I love her music. I listen to the words. They're really good lyrics. You should listen to them. They're about being true to yourself and making good choices like you want me to do."

Mom laughed a little and patted my hand. "I almost forgot this is all about Lola Bay."

I smiled back.

"You should listen to some more of those Lola Bay songs about good choices. And think about not letting something like this happen again. Okay?"

"Okay, Mom. Will you listen to some songs with me?"

"Sure."

✦✧✦

Monday morning, I found Dana at school. "Has your mom said anything?" I asked.

"No. But if your mom tells my mom, it will be bad."

"I don't think she will. She just gave me a big lecture about making good choices. And she listened to Lola Bay songs with me."

"Really? Wow. Cool."

"Have you seen Paige or Salima?" I asked.

"Not yet. And I haven't heard anything, but it's only a matter of time."

"It's kind of like it didn't really happen," I said.

She gave me one of her *you-are-so-immature* looks. "Oh, it happened all right. You'll see."

By lunchtime, it was school news, but not as bad as I feared it would be. I put a hamburger and French fries on my tray and walked toward the tables. Right away, my eyes caught Paige waving at me. I chewed the inside of my cheek as I made my way over. Salima was beaming and bouncing her hair around with its faint rainbow hues. I sat down, and before I could say anything, Lydia Hale came over.

"Salima, your hair is so cool. I heard Callie did it."

Callie sat up with authority. "I did. With special pens. I won the Lola Bay Lyrics Contest."

"She didn't win," said Salima. "I lost."

"It's not a contest, it's a game," said Paige. "I lost. Can you see my chameleon skin?"

"You lost?" asked Lydia.

"Yes," explained Callie. "To lose is to kind of win. You get your hair and eyes and nails done."

"How do you play?" asked Lydia.

"Oh, you have to be a member of the Unofficial Lola Bay Fan Club," said Bethany as she crowded into the table.

"How do you join?" Lydia asked.

"Ask Iris," said Callie. "She's president."

I was speechless. I didn't know what to say.

"Can I join, Iris?" asked Lydia.

"I have to talk to Dana. She's the vice president. I'll let you know."

Lydia touched a strand of Salima's hair, then looked closely at Paige's cheek. "I think a lot of kids are going to want to join."

As she walked away, Bethany said to her, "You better memorize all the Lola Bay lyrics."

"Iris." Salima tapped my tray with her fork. "Iris, did you bring the membership cards with you?"

The easy answer was no, but I really wanted to know how this flip-flop had occurred. "I don't have them. I thought you all decided you didn't want to join."

"That was before we realized how really cool it was and how all we have to do is bring our own makeup and stuff to the meeting," Bethany said. "Then we don't have to use art supplies that give your mother a nervous breakdown!"

"I want to lose next time," said Callie.

The table broke out in giggles.

Some girl I didn't know walked by the table and gave Salima a thumbs-up and she blushed.

I didn't know what to do. My voice sounded pinched when I said, "I'll talk to Dana."

I used all forty-five minutes of Studio Arts to think about how to tell Dana. When we were walking out, I spilled it all.

She put her fingertips to her temples like she had a headache. "No," she said. "No. No. No. No. No. No."

I breathed a huge sigh of relief. It was good to have her make the decision to turn them down. While I had been drawing manga Lola Bay, I'd had daydream night-mares about what would happen if the Unofficial Lola Bay Fan Club turned into a makeup and hairstyling club where people wanted to lose the Lyrics Game so they could get their nails done.

"At least the whole school thinks it was a cool thing, not a bad thing," I said as we walked down the hall.

"There is that," Dana said. She walked with her usual composure, maybe even a little more pride. I don't think she would have looked so good if the school gossip had gone the other way.

"What do you think will happen when we tell them no?" I asked. I was afraid she was going to make me tell them.

She stopped and leaned against the lockers. "Iris. I think we agree the club should be limited to us, right?"

"Right."

"And you are the president, right?"

"Right."

"So you need to have a positive attitude and tell them that for right now, until we work out the new rules, mem-bership is closed. We'll let them know when it's open again. They'll be the first." She looked deep into my eyes to see if I understood what she had just said.

It was brilliant. It was something I probably would

have thought of if I was in seventh grade. "That's perfect. I can do that."

"Good. Do it."

When I told them at the end of the day, they were like, "Oh. Okay," which surprised and relieved me after all the fuss.

The next afternoon, I was hurrying past the choir room when a green sheet of paper on the floor caught my eye. My foot trapped the corner of it and I read:

OFFICIAL LOLA BAY FAN CLUB MEMBERSHIP DRIVE
Join the one and only Official Lola Bay Fan Club and enter the LOLA BAY LYRICS CONTEST! Win cool Lola Bay swag for knowing all the lyrics to Lola Bay's songs.

If a person's blood could roar in their ears, that's what mine did. Howling and baying over Melanie Fish Face stealing our Lyrics Game idea. I was having trouble lifting my foot off the paper to pick it up. Kids began bumping into me.

"You look like you've seen a ghost," said Dana, appearing at my side.

I pointed down to the green paper.

She bent over and grabbed it. Before it was fully at eye level, she was crunching it into a ball. Daggers were shooting from her eyes. "That was my idea. Me, my, mine. She stole my game!"

"She can't do this!" I cried.

Dana looked at me through steely eyes. "Well, it won't go unaddressed."

As if that wasn't enough, at lunchtime, Melanie Fish Face was quoted all over school as saying she had been personally contacted by the Official Lola Bay Fan Club and told that Lola Bay was extending her concert tour dates to include Chicago on November 11 and 12, *and* that the Minnesota club members were getting special rates on tickets and airfare to the concert.

By the end of the day, Bethany, Callie, Salima, and Paige were members of the official club.

$\div$11$\div$

BACK UNDER CONTROL—NOT

MELANIE FISH FACE really did have advance notice, because an official press release didn't come out until 4:00 p.m. the next day. Dana came to my house after school, and her mood was positively electric.

She handed me a printout of the release. "We have to go! We can't let Fish Face and the Imitators and Bethany, Callie, Salima, and Paige go and we're not there. It would be . . . so unfair. So wrong."

I agreed. I was still angry, and now I was desperate to go to the concert. "What if it's sold out already?"

"What if it's not?"

"The tickets have to be super-expensive."

"I think the closer you get to the concert, the cheaper

they get because they want to sell them all," Dana argued.

I looked at her to see if she was serious. Because she was a year older, it was possible she knew stuff I didn't know. Still, it sounded wrong. "Uh, I don't think so. I think the closer you get to the concert date, the fewer there are, and the more expensive the ones that're left are."

"Oh my gosh. Let's just look." Dana sat down in front of my laptop. With a few clicks, she was on the page for Lola Bay concert dates.

Even if we couldn't go, and I was pretty sure we couldn't, I was prepared to die of grief if it was already sold out.

She clicked on Chicago, Saturday, November 12, and a color-coded seating plan popped up. "Yes!" she screamed, and pumped her fist.

I gasped. "I don't believe it!"

Dana spun around and grabbed my arms. She was almost crying, she was so happy. "Let's buy tickets."

"I don't have any money. Do you?"

She looked at me and lowered her voice. "No, but do you have a credit card?"

"Are you kidding me? No, I don't have a credit card. Do you?"

"No." Dana drummed her French-manicured nails on the desktop. "Your parents must have a card we could use."

I laughed. "Yours too."

She stiffened. "Sure they do, but my mom's at work and my dad is sleeping . . . at my house, so . . ."

"So, what? Use my parents' credit card? If I ask my mom for her credit card, she'll ask me what for, and if I tell her it's to buy Lola Bay concert tickets in Chicago, she'll laugh her head off."

"Don't ask her."

I squinted. "What?"

Dana shrugged.

"Are you saying use the card without asking her?"

She blinked at me like she was insulted. "It's the only way to get the tickets before they're gone. We'll pay your parents back, for sure."

"With what money?" I looked over at my bed, to my backpack, which held my school ID and $17. I could afford two trips to Pizza Papa's.

Dana didn't miss a beat. "We'll sell stuff."

"We'd have to sell a lot of stuff. What would we sell? Cookies? Like at church?"

She squirmed in her seat. "Whatever we want. Don't worry about that now. We'll figure it out. Just go get the card and let's buy the tickets before they're sold out." She nudged my shoulder. "Hurry."

It only took me a few seconds to realize she was right. If we didn't buy the tickets now, they would be gone. And if they were gone, everyone would be there but us. And we could find a way to pay my parents back. The very idea of the evil, game-stealing Melanie Fisher being there with Lola Bay and not us made me furious.

"We need to be there," she urged.

I nodded and pushed off my seat. "Stay here."

I opened my bedroom door a crack and listened for voices. They were in the family room playing some game. They wouldn't be able to hear me. I knew it was silly, but I snuck with my back against the wall all the way to the top of the stairs. I knew exactly where my mom's purse was—on the shelf in the kitchen where she dropped it every day when she came home. It was past snack time, so they wouldn't be going into the kitchen. One deep breath later, I was down the stairs, through the kitchen, and staring at the credit cards in her wallet.

With my heart racing like hummingbird wings, I wiggled one out, zoomed back up to my room, and slammed into my chair, breathless.

Dana reached for it, but I said, "Wait. Put your hand over your heart and repeat after me: I, Dana Dean."

Dana rolled her eyes, but she did it. "I, Dana Dean."

"Swear with Iris Underwood on our offices as president and vice president of the Unofficial Lola Bay Fan Club."

She repeated, "Swear with Iris Underwood on our

offices as president and vice president of the Unofficial Lola Bay Fan Club."

"That we will pay back every cent of the money we use from this card to buy Lola Bay concert tickets."

She repeated, "That we will pay back every cent of the money we use from this card to buy Lola Bay concert tickets."

I handed over the credit card with a solemn expression on my face. We picked seats that cost $125 each plus some taxes and fees. The total was almost $300. Dana put in all the numbers and clicked Purchase. It was all too easy. I wondered when the tickets would show up on the credit card bill.

She must have read my mind because she gave me a hug and said, "Don't worry, we'll pay it back before they even know." She pressed the card into my hand, and I ran downstairs and tucked it back into the wallet.

The whole time, I thought about how this was a good choice because tickets would sell out and we had to act now, and we were going to pay it all back.

I stood at the printer waiting for the tickets to spit out. Three hundred dollars felt like a million, but Dana was so sure we'd figure it out that I relaxed.

We threw ourselves into planning what we would wear to the concert. She was so happy. It made me feel like I'd done something good for her. I also got a thrill imagining being in our seats at the concert and having the music go straight from Lola Bay's microphone to our ears, her voice making us melt.

✦ ✦ ✦

Dana and I floated through the next two days, talking about the concert. That is, until Thursday, when Melanie Fish Face ruined it.

"Oh, Iris, Iris Underwood," Melanie yelled from her position as queen of her lunch table.

Her voice had the power to silence the taco eating and milk slurping. I paused as I was walking to dump my tray but didn't look at her.

"I suppose you've heard about the Chicago concert dates?"

I turned and said, "I have. And Dana and I are going." It was a loaded answer, since we had tickets but I wasn't sure if we were going to get to use them.

Then Melanie and the Imitators did something that completely messed up my mind. They reached into their backpacks and pulled out Lola Bay faces on Popsicle sticks and held them in front of their heads. A table full of Lola Bay smiles danced in front of me, along with the sickening smell of tacos.

I felt woozy. I thought I was going to faint.

The sound of hoots snapped me out of it. The rest

of the kids in the cafeteria were pointing at them and laughing.

Melanie lowered her Lola Bay face and reached into her backpack and started pulling things out. "If you were official, Iris, you would have these too. A new black concert tee, a concert tour button, a swag ribbon, a PopSocket, a light stick for when she sings 'Break Me, Wake Me' . . . But wait . . . You're not official. You're in a club with loser Dana. Oh well. Never mind."

I willed my feet to move. This time they obeyed and took me out of the cafeteria and to my locker, which I kicked until my toe hurt.

I kicked the locker because I wanted all the official stuff. I kicked the locker because I should have had all the official stuff. I kicked the locker because I didn't want mean Melanie Fish Face and the Imitators to have any of it. I kicked the locker just because.

Friday, something else big happened. Lola Bay announced a new product called LB Faux Ink. She had designed new versions of her logo as fake tattoos, and you could order them at her merch store. She said in an interview, "I don't permanently do anything. I decorate, but if I change my mind, I wipe it clean and start over."

I assumed Melanie Fish Face and the Imitators all

ordered theirs immediately. Then at the lunch table, Callie and Salima said the Official Lola Bay Fan Club was overnighting enough free ones for the whole club.

The next day, Saturday, I was merch-crabby when Dana showed up at my house. She wanted to go straight to the computer. "Let's get some LB Faux Ink tattoos."

"It depends on how much they cost," I said.

"We'll need them for Chicago. It's part of the whole concert thing."

"Still, we don't have the money."

I suddenly realized she had dumped a big stack of *Music Scene* magazines on my bed. They each had a different picture of Lola Bay on the cover.

"Oh my gosh, where'd you get these?" I asked.

"From the library."

"Did you check them out?"

"No, dude. Look at them, Iris. They're old and worn out. Someone left them in the donations box. You can just take them."

I wasn't sure about that. "Oh. I thought if someone donated books and stuff, the library put their name on it and put it on the shelves to check out."

"Come on, let's go to the Lola Bay site. Stop worrying about the stupid magazines. If I hadn't taken them, Melanie Fish Face would have. Isn't it better that we have them?"

I spun around and faced her. My face felt flushed. I launched. "I don't want to look at the magazines you took from the donation box, even if you kept Melanie Fish Face from getting them, and I don't want to go to the Lola Bay site."

"What are you so crabby about? Seriously, Iris, don't you think we should have more flash than game-stealing Melanie Fish Face? Don't you?"

I flopped onto my bed. She knew me so well. "Yes. Yes, I do."

Dana sat down at my computer like it was a grand piano. "I was in the computer lab today, doing you a big favor."

I sat up. "What?"

"Just a little research on how these online sale sites are set up. I did it for a research paper. Wink, wink."

This time, instead of going to Lola Bay's website, she navigated to the official fan club site. She clicked on Merch.

"What do we want?"

"What do you mean?"

"Look. What do we want? T-shirts, light sticks, faces on sticks, PopSockets, tote bags, dog collars, LB tattoos?"

"I don't have a dog."

"Neither do I. Let's get two of everything else."

It was so exciting shopping for Lola Bay things, I

almost forgot we had the same problem as the tickets. How would we pay for them?

"Hey, we can't afford this. We haven't even started figuring out how to pay my parents back for the tickets."

"I promise I'll do that. I have a plan. This stuff, I can make it so it's free."

"How's that?"

"Just watch."

I watched, but I didn't follow what was going on. It was too fast. Her fingers flew over the keys. Lines of code scrolled by at lightning speed, moving in blocks. The only thing I recognized was a mailing address.

"Whose address is that?" I asked.

"It's a couple blocks from my house. They're never home, and I have Amazon packages sent to their back porch all the time. It's easy: You just give Amazon the directions where to put it." Dana smiled. "Comprende?"

Marbles were falling into slots in my head. Free stuff. Delivered to a neighbor who was never home, in a spot they would never look, so her parents would never know.

She laughed at my expression. "Yes. I'm kind of good at this."

"So, you go through the pay screen the same way you went through the school library wall?"

"Yes, kind of. You saw. The books are still in the library, and if the Lola Bay Fan Club knew we were actually the original fan club here, they would have sent this stuff to us too. They give it out like candy to every club all over the world. So it's, like, free to true fans."

She was right about the library books that we'd checked out to Melanie. They were still on the shelves. And it was technically true that we should have been given the free merch instead of Melanie. And we were true fans.

"Wait a minute. If it's free stuff, why do you have to send it to some stranger's back porch?"

"Duh. It's not free to just anyone. Regular people would have to pay for it. We're not exactly the official fan club, right? We're sort of regular people. We just *would have been* the official fan club if it hadn't been stolen from us. Right?"

I thought about this for a second, and I still didn't understand. Then that little thing that was gnawing at my gut that was also making me cranky pushed me to say, "But wait. We still have to pay my parents back for the tickets. When are we going to do that?"

Dana's brow narrowed, and her voice sharpened. "I can't talk to you when you're being whiny. I said we'd pay them back and we will. I have a plan."

"What plan? And when?"

"When I'm ready. Sheesh."

I sat on the bed and picked up a magazine. My brain

was connecting dots. They weren't all making sense, but they were connected. I blurted out, "Is this why you don't have your own computer and why you can't be online on your phone?"

She laughed. "Bingo. My mom is the internet police. She checked my search history and shut me off."

"Is that why you hate her?" Uh-oh. That slipped out.

Dana's French-manicured fingertips paused on the keyboard. "What?"

Now I felt like I had to explain. "I came over to your house a couple Sundays ago, and before I got to the door, you and your mom were in the driveway going to the gym. I overheard your conversation and I didn't want to interrupt, so I—"

"So you spied on me? And how come you could hear me but I couldn't see you? Where were you? Hiding?"

"I didn't want to interrupt. I was trying to be polite—"

"How is it polite to listen in on a conversation that isn't yours?"

"I wasn't listening."

"I guess you were!" Dana headed for the bedroom door. "I thought we were friends. I just got you free swag."

My voice came out a little like I was pleading. "We are."

"I thought I could trust you."

"You can. I just felt bad about how your mom treated you."

She spun on me. "No, you didn't, Iris. You're just nosy. Well, excuse me if that's none of your business. Are you going to go blab that around school now? Dana's mother is a witch?"

My tongue struggled to form words.

She shook her head and left.

"No!" I called after her. "No, I would never! Don't go!"

The silence hurt my ears. I didn't move.

The twins burst through my door, and I screamed, "GET OUT OF MY ROOM!"

✦ ✦ ✦

Uggghhh! I just wanted a friend who was like me. I wanted a friend who liked what I liked. I wanted a friend who didn't give up on Lola Bay to play volleyball or hate her mother or sneak into websites. I just wanted a normal fan club. And the Unofficial Lola Bay Fan Club was far from normal.

Downstairs, Mom was banging around in the kitchen starting dinner. I decided to go down and do something boringly normal and help her.

"Oh, Iris, would you set the table?" she asked when I walked in.

"Sure." Ian and Echo were already in their chairs with forks and spoons to occupy them. "Hey, guys, want to set the table with me?"

"I can set the table," said Echo.

"Here, you fold the napkin for Dad."

"I fold the napkins," Ian said.

"You fold the napkin for Mom," I told him.

Somehow, without anyone busting out crying, we got the table set.

"How was your day?" Mom asked me as she stood over the sink peeling carrots.

How was my day? That was hard to answer. So much had just happened in the last hour. I whispered without conviction, "It was okay."

Mom looked over her shoulder at me with her eyebrows raised. "Oh yeah? Anything happen?"

"No."

She went from peeling to chopping. The twins were now wearing the napkins on their heads.

"Mom. Did you ever donate anything?"

"Sure. Like to the Family Shelter Program? We've donated old clothes, and I just dropped off a box of baby clothes. Why? Do have something you want to donate?"

"Do you think it's stealing if you take something that's been . . . donated?"

She went still and answered in her teacher voice. "Like what? What kind of something?"

"Oh, like, say you were walking by the Family Shelter Program donations trailer and there was a bike left there. Do you think it would be stealing to take it before the Family Shelter people took it inside?"

She laid her knife down and looked at me. "That's an interesting question, Iris. What do you think?"

"MOM. I'm asking you what *you* think."

"Did you take something that was sitting by the Family Shelter Program trailer?"

"NO. It's just a question. Can't you just answer the question?"

"I'll answer it this way: Was the bike left there for you?"

I hated when she did this. It was another *choices* talk. But I knew the perfectly technical answer to this. "No, it was left for someone who didn't have a bike. But if I was someone who didn't have a bike, then it could be for someone like me. Oh, never mind."

"Iris? Did you take something?"

"No."

I ran upstairs, but I heard her call out, "Iris? Is there something you need to tell me?"

"NOOOOOOOOOOOOOOO!"

12

THE DEPTHS OF DESPAIR

ONCE AGAIN, DANA ignored me at school. Her cute skirts would swish every time she saw me and turned the other way. It was extreme punishment.

Leeza was with Regina and the volleyball gang, and Ted. Paige, Callie, Bethany, and Salima were with Melanie Fish Face, although she didn't let them sit at her lunch table.

I was left with me, myself, and I, and I kept daydreaming nightmares.

I didn't know what I was going to do. I had no idea how to pay back my parents. Every ounce of enthusiasm I had for the concert was draining away while everyone else's was soaring. When Melanie Fish Face and the Imitators got their tattoos, I sobbed in the last stall in the girls' bathroom.

Soon, I found myself scouring the school for Dana, hoping to bump into her and have a chance to make things right.

It took four days, but I finally caught her in the computer lab and slid into the seat next to her.

She knew I was there, because she moved her things away from me. She had an LB tattoo on the inside of her wrist. It hurt just to see it.

I didn't know quite how to start.

She scrolled and clicked on Lola Bay news. That hurt even more. We usually did that together.

Then she surprised me and said, "Look. Lola Bay is going to be on the *Tonight Show*. We can see it on YouTube."

What? A glimmer of hope. She said *we*.

"Are you still mad?" I squeaked.

"Of course I'm still mad. Are you expecting me to forgive you again?"

I said my sort-of-planned speech. "Yes. Because you know I wasn't really spying. I was stuck and didn't know what to do. I didn't want to butt in, and it turned out looking like I was spying. But I wasn't."

She turned to me with her lips pursed. "I suppose I

can give you another chance. But you have to learn to make better choices, Iris. You've done some really imma-ture sixth-grade stuff."

Sheesh, she sounded like my mom with the choices thing. I was getting a little sick of people lecturing me about that. I was not the same little kid from last summer. I was a different girl, and I didn't think all my choices were the worst in the world.

"Iris, I'm going to forgive you, but don't do that again."

"I guess if I come to your house and you're in the driveway fighting with your mom, I'll just go away."

"Good choice. She's harsh. You do not want to tangle with her."

I wanted desperately to ask, *Is that why you hate her?* But I didn't want to start the fight all over again. She must have seen the question in my eyes.

"I don't hate her all the time. Just when she does mean stuff to me and cares only about her stupid job and what people think of her."

I kept my mouth shut and didn't say that I thought she also cared a lot about what people thought of her. I congratulated myself on that good choice.

"So, do you want the good news?" Dana asked.

"Yes!"

"I figured out how we're going to pay your parents back."

"You did? How?"

"I'll show you when we're in your room and I can use your computer."

"Can you show me here?" I pointed to the school computer.

"Nope. I don't have time now. I could stay over Saturday if you want and we can plan it all out."

"Wow. Sure. That would be great." Relief flowed through me. I wondered if we were making a million bracelets to sell or what.

✦✧✦

I had to beg Mom a little bit about Dana staying over on such short notice. And she insisted on calling her parents, like we were little kids, which was embarrassing.

Finally, it was all worked out, and it seemed like an eternity until the next day.

"Tell me!" I demanded when Dana got to my house late Saturday afternoon.

"Let's wait until after dinner," she said with a sly look. "When it's dark. It's really good."

"OMG. Stop teasing me."

Luckily, Mom was letting us eat in my room like a

picnic. I picked at my chicken nuggets, and Dana made me try to guess her plan.

"Bracelets?"

"No."

"Cookies?"

"No. No cooking."

"Headbands?"

"No. No sewing."

"Birdhouses."

"No hammering and nailing."

"WELL, WHAT THEN?"

"Turn off the lights."

Dana finally did what she did best. She positioned herself at my laptop, powered it up, and clicked and clicked and clicked until I saw flashes of rainbow colors and ripples of gold.

"Ta-da. It's a fundraising site. Strangers give you money."

"What? Like for people who have cancer?"

"More than that. It's crowdfunding, kick-starting. You know."

She pointed to the screen. It said "What's Your Dream?" She clicked on Dreams.

There were hundreds, maybe thousands, of pages of individual people with their dreams and how much money they needed to make them come true, like *Help Me Learn to Surf—$5,000*, *Help Me Make a Movie—$50,000*, *Help Me Learn Pottery—$275*.

"I mean, really." Dana sat up on her knees in the chair. "Look at this guy. He wants to take his three-legged dog to swimming lessons."

We searched around the site. People were asking for money for stupid things like making potato salad. Lola Bay concert tickets seemed more important than potato salad.

I felt a surge of excitement. *Help Me Learn Pottery— $275* gave me hope.

Dana moved the cursor over the Start tab and wiggled it around. The cursor blinked. She leaned forward and looked at me for my okay. The cursor continued to blink.

I chewed my lip. I imagined a page saying, *Send two girls to the Lola Bay concert! We're her biggest fans.* Wasn't a Lola Bay concert as important as a three-legged dog taking swimming lessons?

I glazed over, thinking about people choosing between the three-legged dog and us.

Dana waved her hand in front of my eyes. "Iris. Come on. This is how we pay your parents back for the tickets."

I took a deep breath. "Ready."

She beamed and clicked on Start. The cursor blinked in the Name box. She typed in the first name field *IRI*—

"Hey, wait." I hadn't expected to see my name on the screen. "Why my name? Can't we be anonymous?"

"Obviously you can't be anonymous when you sign up, or they wouldn't put a place for a name. Money's involved. They have to know who to pay. We may not have to put names on the public page. We could call ourselves Lola Bay Fangirls or something."

That seemed reasonable to me. "Okay. Go ahead."

She typed in my name and hit Enter. The cursor jumped to the Address field.

"I thought you were going to put in both of our names."

"I never knew a person who put up such a fuss about getting free money. Don't be a baby. You need to put in your address."

I blocked out the sound of the furnace kicking on and the feel of warm air on my feet. "No. You put in your address."

She swallowed, closed her eyes, then leaned close to me and whispered, "First of all, the address has to match the name and the credit card, and second of all, I can't, because . . ." She looked at me like *I already told you.* "I'm not even supposed to be online. So I dare you. I triple dare you to get rich."

Now she was being silly. She raised her hands in the air like, *So?*

Dana was older than me, and smarter than me, and had all kinds of experience that I didn't have. I didn't want another week of her avoiding me.

I pulled my chair closer to hers. "Okay, go ahead and use my address."

She clicked, and the cursor jumped to Title of Page. She typed in *Help Me Go to the Lola Bay Concert!*

"Shouldn't it say help *us* go to the concert?"

"It only knows you."

Ha! I laughed. "What do you mean, it only knows me?"

"I mean, you are the only person listed on the site, silly."

The cursor skipped to Amount You Wish to Raise, and blinked. Before I could say anything, Dana typed in *$5,000* and pressed Enter.

I was shocked. "We don't need that much."

"Are you kidding? We need to travel to Chicago and stay in a hotel and eat."

"Won't it seem like too much money for just one person?"

"People don't know where you're coming from, so they don't really know how much it costs."

"But my address is there."

"I don't think the public sees that."

The cursor jumped to a field that asked How Do You Wish to Receive Your Donations? There were options like PayPal and Visa, Mastercard, and AmEx.

Dana took a scrap of paper out of her pocket. "See, this is how we pay your parents back. The donations go straight to their credit card."

I liked that they would be paid back, but I was more focused on the piece of paper. "Wait a minute. What's that?"

"It's the credit card number."

"You wrote it down? Why?" Hair prickled the back of my neck. "You shouldn't have kept that number. I didn't say you could keep that number."

I expected her to apologize. But she didn't. She shrugged it off. "I knew we'd need it to pay them back, and I didn't think it made any sense sending you back to your mom's purse. What's the big deal?"

I was trying to think of what the big deal was since we really did need the card number to pay them back. Next we had to Click Here and Read and Accept Terms and Conditions. Dana clicked and clicked and scrolled to the bottom and hit Accept.

The next thing I knew she'd saved the page, entered a username and password, and written it down on another scrap of paper.

I was about to ask her for the username and password when there was a knock at the door.

"Good night, girls," Dad said without opening it.

Dana shut down the computer.

"Aren't we going to watch our page?" I asked.

"It's boring until the money starts coming in. Wait until tomorrow morning. Just wait."

13

DRAMATIC TURN OF EVENTS

I WOKE UP Sunday morning to Dana hunched over my computer with a strained expression on her face.

"What? Do we have any donations?" I threw off my covers, ran across the room, and leaned over her shoulder.

She shook her head. "Not yet."

That's when I saw it. My picture on our page. I reached out and touched the screen. Chills ran up my spine. "How did that get there?"

"It will get more donations if it's personal."

"It's already personal. It has my name!"

"Now it's even more personal. Pictures say more than words." She closed the page. "I have to go. My mom will be here to pick me up any second, and she hates to wait."

"Don't you want breakfast?"

"No time."

She wasn't kidding. Five minutes later, Dana was flying down the stairs to the front door.

She passed my mom, who was standing at the bottom holding two cinnamon muffins. "Don't you want something to eat?"

She ignored the question. "Thanks for letting me stay." She reached for the door. "My mom is picking me up right now."

Mom and I followed her to the door.

Dana ran to the waiting car and jumped in. She jammed her duffel bag in with her.

When they were gone, without looking at me, Mom handed me a muffin, which I immediately took upstairs and munched on while I stared at the fundraising page.

At lunchtime, Mom called me to come down, but I didn't move until the third time she called. My eyes were still fixed on the tally window under the golden bucket on our page, waiting for a coin to drop in and make an electronic shimmer.

The more I watched it, the more convinced I became that money would start to flood in. If you believed what they said on the site, it reached millions of wealthy people looking for a way to do good deeds. A nurse raised $125,352 for a cancer wing at the children's hospital, and a college student raised $530,063 for her documentary movie about the attachment baby penguins form to humans, and a kid from Minnesota whose parents were both in the army raised $19,233 to train for the Olympic luge team.

I closed my computer and my door and ran down to the kitchen.

Mom was still eating and cleaning up after the twins while talking to Dad. "Just ran out without eating a thing."

My breath caught. I knew that kind of talk might mean something bad about Dana. I grabbed half of a grilled cheese sandwich. It wasn't my favorite, but eating what had been fixed seemed like a good idea.

Dad drank his coffee. "What do you mean?"

Mom wiped Echo's face. "I don't know. She's not very sociable. Or polite, really."

"Yeah, those muffin rules are pretty strict," said Dad. He had a glint in his eye.

She rolled her eyes and took the wet towel to Ian's sticky hands. "For heaven's sake. Am I not entitled to an observation?"

Dad looked at me. "What do you think, Iris? Unsociable or impolite?"

I felt pushed into a corner. "Is it a crime to not be hungry? How unfair to Dana. Did you want her to make her mother wait in the car while she ate a muffin she didn't want?"

He smiled. "Marnie, you're being unfair to Dana."

She stabbed her hand into her hip and gave him a *you're not helping* look.

I snorted.

Dad jumped in without joking. "Hang on, Iris. We're just interested in what kind of friends you hang out with. That's fair, especially after the glitter-eyelid thing."

"Ugh. How many times do I have to tell you? She didn't do the glitter, or the hair. She read the rules. She's fine. She wasn't hungry. She wasn't rude." I sighed and ran back upstairs, thinking maybe she was a teeny bit rude.

An hour later, my eyeballs were still glued to the empty bucket.

"IRIS?" Mom yelled.

"WHAT?"

"Echo can't find Rosie. Can you help her look?"

"Rosie's probably under her bed."

"Can you help her?"

"Can't she look?"

"IRIS!"

"COMING."

Rosie the gopher was under the bed, as I predicted. I didn't mind helping so much when I saw the relief on Echo's face and how hard she hugged that raggedy thing. Two seconds later, she was hitting Ian over the head with it. Oh well. Toddlers.

I went back to the bucket. There was nothing to be done but wait. So I waited.

Then, when I was just finishing my homework, my ears perked to a jingling, tinkling sound!

The bucket was shimmering, and we had gotten $5 from Anonymous.

My heart soared. Five dollars was something. We needed a whole lot more, but it was a start.

Monday morning, I was ready for school early. I couldn't wait to tell Dana that we had a donation. Dad, on the other hand, needed help. Echo was stretched out over the bottom three steps in a state of extreme distress, and Dad was struggling to put on her shoes. I jumped to make lunches. While I was slapping the last PB&J sandwich closed, my eye caught Ian scribbling in my math book and I groaned.

Dad hustled Echo into the kitchen and saw the lunch

bags. "Thank you, Iris. You are the best." Then he saw Ian scribbling in my book. "Oh no. Ian. Well, nothing we can do about it now. Water under the bridge."

That's what he always said about things that couldn't be fixed. Water under the stupid bridge. I finished the lunches, threw my book into my backpack, and ran for the bus.

I plopped down next to Leeza.

"Rah, I heard you came over," she said.

"Uh-huh. Like a week ago."

"So?"

"So nothing. I just came over."

"Sorry I wasn't there. The team went out for pizza."

"Yeah, that's what your mom said."

I almost added *I just wanted to hang out*, but before I could, she said, "Couldn't Dana come over?"

That was kind of snotty. I didn't say anything. I sulked the rest of the ride. Here I'd been so excited about our $5, and now I was mad at Leeza.

I didn't see Dana until Studio Arts, and I tried to tell her that we had $5 by raising my hand with all five fingers spread. She kept shrugging, like, *What?*

After the bell rang and we were out in the hall,

I whispered, "Five dollars! Last night Anonymous contributed five dollars."

She pumped her fist.

✦ ✦ ✦

After the last bell, we waded into the mass of bodies streaming toward the line of buses and climbed aboard #16B. I headed for my regular seat, and there was Leeza.

"What? No practice today?" I said. "I thought you practiced Mondays and Thursdays."

Dana was also surprised. She'd expected to sit with me. She sat behind us.

Leeza's thumbs were working on a text. She didn't look up. "Uh, yeah. Not today. Schedule change this week."

Dante, a Goth kid, banged my elbow as he jostled down the aisle.

A shadow over my shoulder told me Dana was reading Leeza's phone.

"Stop skulking, Dana!" Leeza snapped.

Dana thumped the back of Leeza's head with her perfect fingers. I cringed.

"Stop it!" Leeza leaned forward for protection. At the same time, she gave me a *what the heck?* expression. I knew she wouldn't get into an argument with Dana. It wasn't like her.

I watched YouTube videos of Lola Bay on my phone for the rest of the ride. Dana bounced her red boot against the bottom of the seat.

Finally, we all got off at our stop. Dana and I slammed into the house and pounded up the stairs.

"IRIS?" Mom called from the dining room.

I stopped midstep but waved Dana on to my room. "WHAT?"

"Would you mind getting the twins their snack?"

"In a minute, okay? We have to do something."

"We?" Her irritation that Dana was there cut the air like a knife.

"We, me and Dana. Okay?"

Echo and Ian appeared at the bottom of the steps.

"I want apple and cheese," said Echo.

"I want crackers and grapes," said Ian. He held up six fingers to show me exactly how many he wanted.

"I want grapes," said Echo. She looked at Ian, then held up four fingers.

I was torn between racing to my room and running down to get the twins their snacks. But the bucket called.

"Go to the kitchen, guys," I told them. "I'll be right there."

I almost broke my neck on a plastic truck as I flew into my room. Dana was already on my computer.

"IRIS!" Mom's voice pierced my closed door.

"I have to go get the twins their snack," I told Dana.

She was already in the zone. "Go ahead. I'll pull up the page."

"I'll be right back."

"Shut the door."

I found Mom in the kitchen pulling graham crackers and peanut butter out of the cabinet. Echo and Ian kicked the chair legs and groused about not wanting graham crackers or peanut butter. Mom made an exasperated face, then walked out.

A few minutes later, Dana stuck her head into the kitchen. "Hey, are you coming up or what?"

I put the sticky crackers in front of the twins and ran upstairs.

She pointed at the bucket. "Look at this."

It said $325.

I grabbed Dana's hands and we jumped up and down and squealed.

She pushed me away. "Yuck, you got peanut butter on me!"

14

THINGS LOOK UP

THAT NIGHT IN bed, my mood called for Lola Bay's "My Heart Soars." My parents' credit card was going to be paid back for the concert tickets. I began to believe that two unofficial fangirls might actually go to the Lola Bay concert in Chicago on November 12. It was two and a half weeks away, and there were obviously strangers out there who cared. There was time to work it all out.

I spun fantasies about how we would get a nice hotel and eat meals at fancy restaurants. For the first time, it felt real. Of course, we would need one of our parents to go with us. I figured it wouldn't be either of Dana's since her dad slept during the day and her mom would probably say no just because. It would have to be my mom or dad, and uh-oh! It hit me that we would need another ticket for them, and there probably weren't any more left! I couldn't believe I hadn't thought of this sooner.

I ran to the computer and pulled up the concert site. Ack! SOLD OUT!

Sold out. Sold out. Sold out. I couldn't believe it. I ran my fingers down my cheeks and stretched my face out.

I zombied back into bed and tried to think of what to do. Suddenly, I realized an adult probably wouldn't want to actually *go* to the concert. They could wait outside. Or they could drop us off and pick us up. That would work. We'd get a really nice hotel room so they could watch movies while they waited. I started to relax. This would all work out. They would be surprised and proud of me and Dana for figuring out how to raise the money to travel and for a nice hotel room.

✦✧✦

"Look at this." Dana handed me a folded paper the next day before Studio Arts. "Don't let anyone see it."

When Ms. Wells wasn't near me, I unfolded it. It was a spreadsheet with all the other costs of our trip: two round-trip bus tickets, a night in a hotel, bus to hotel and back, taxi from hotel to concert and back, and food. It added up to $750. I nearly fainted with joy. That was so much less than $5,000. I looked across the room at her, and she gave me a thumbs-up. My mind was buzzing so fast the whole class that I made my manga eyes too big.

On the way down the hall, Dana gave me an encouraging smile and said, "We can so do this. We already have enough to pay for the tickets—all we need is $750 more."

"I thought we would have to take a plane," I said.

"Bus is less expensive and less hassle."

"I get that. But what if my parents drove instead of us taking a bus? Then there would only be gas."

She squinted like she was considering this. "Why not have your mom or dad relax and enjoy the trip and not have the hassle of driving in Chicago? It's like a vacation. We'll get another bus ticket."

That seemed right. "I looked last night. There are no more concert tickets, so my mom or dad will have to stay at the hotel while we're at the concert, so it has to be a nice one."

Dana said, "Sure. No problem."

I took a deep breath. It was all coming together.

Then she asked, "Do you really think one of your parents will go with us to Chicago?"

"Get out of the way, dorks!" Three soccer players pushed around us.

"Why? Do you think *yours* will?" I said.

Dana stopped hard, and fifteen kids piled up behind her. She grabbed my arm and pulled me to the lockers.

I yanked my arm back. "I figured your parents wouldn't do it, so it would have to be mine."

Dana sighed in frustration. "I don't know. They might."

"It will have to be one of our parents, obviously. Because we can't go alone."

She looked down the hall like she was thinking about how to say something, and then she turned back to me. "Okay. Let's not ask your parents yet. I think I may be able to get my dad to do it. Okay? He's a musician, after all. He likes Lola Bay."

Wow. This surprised me. "Okay. I guess."

"Promise not to ask your parents, okay? Not before I can talk to him."

"Sure. Okay. Meet me at my house after school. Let's see how much we have in the bucket."

On the way home, I thought about the budget and made a mental note to remind her to add another bus ticket.

✦✦✦

Two days went by without another shimmering contribution to our bucket. It was Thursday afternoon. Dana grumped and said she wasn't coming over after school. There was still lots of time—sixteen days until the concert. I kept my hopes up.

At dinner, Dad was hopping around, setting the table and making jokes.

"I've got a surprise for everyone," he said as he sat down. "It's a goody."

Uh-oh. Dad thought a lecture on Odysseus and the wine-dark sea was a goody.

I prepared to act interested. I wanted him to stay in a good mood. With teachers for parents, you always needed a well-thought-out plan, and I had one.

"I got tickets for the whole family to go to the Festival of Mythological Gods and Goddesses at the College of Humanities!" He paused and waited for cheers. He wasn't going to get a reaction from the twins, so it was up to me and Mom.

"When?" Mom asked like he better not come up with the wrong answer.

"Saturday the twelfth," he replied as he scooped mac and cheese onto the twins' plates.

WHAT! My head exploded. I tried to form words, but they kept talking.

"As in the weekend before my high school reunion?" Mom's right eyebrow went up.

"Mm-hmm." Dad slowed his spooning action a little but kept going. I think he realized the complication.

"So, when are we going to prep everything for your mother for when we're away? I can't spend all Saturday at your Greek festival, then teach all week, then leave Friday night."

"Can't we get things ready on Sunday?" he asked.

"Don't try and schedule me." Mom's irritation rose.

OH MY GOSH! My brains were scrambled. *Speak up,* I told myself. *No, don't say anything yet. Wait until we know if Dana's dad can take us.* I promised I'd wait.

"It's not *my* Greek festival, Marnie." His joy over the gods and goddesses fizzled. "But I see your point."

Mom wiped her mouth with a napkin. "Maybe we could ask your mother to go with you and the kids to the festival. That way I can get everything organized."

Dad's face brightened. "Excellent idea, my dear." He leaned over and squeezed her hand, and she softened.

My plan to go to the concert was crumbling like a Greek ruin. I found my voice in spite of myself. "You mean the twelfth as in the Saturday two weeks from this Saturday?"

They both looked at me. "Yes," Dad said. "Why? Do you have something going on? Something at school?"

I was not ready to talk about the concert yet, but I took a deep breath and plowed in anyway. "There is something that Dana and I were going to do. Would it be the end of the world if I missed the festival?"

"What is it?" Mom asked.

Now I was sunk. I never should have mentioned it. If I said *Go to Chicago with Dana and her dad to a Lola Bay concert*, it would start a whole big thing, and Mom would call her parents and start a giant deal before Dana had even asked her dad. That would be bad. I didn't think I had many chances left with Dana.

"Nothing. Never mind."

"Good," said Dad. "You'll love the festival." He totally moved on. He rubbed his hands together and started describing the ancient sports that we'd see, like discus throwing, and how we'd eat something called ambrosia, the food of the gods, and watch a Greek chorus, which he explained does not sing. "And you kids are especially going to love it since you know all about the gods and goddesses!" Then he launched into the story about the noisy mountain nymph.

I tried to hold it together, but I couldn't. My eyes welled up and I ducked my head.

Everyone at the table turned to me. The twins stopped spooning mid-mac.

"Don't cry, Iris," Echo said. She offered me a sticky piece of macaroni.

Mom looked shocked. "Iris!"

A tear rolled down my cheek.

"Okay. Don't get upset." Mom pushed a glass of water closer to me. "Just tell us what it is."

I got up from the table. "I'm not hungry."

I never should have opened my big mouth. I hated the Greek gods.

15

SOMETHING'S DEFINITELY DIFFERENT

IT WAS COLD and drizzly as I climbed on the #16B the next morning.

Leeza slubbed down next to me and nudged my shoulder. "Rah? 'Sup?"

I may have made a sound that came out like an animal growl.

"Whoa. That good, huh?" Leeza pulled out her phone and got sucked in.

I couldn't even concentrate on TikTok videos of people dancing to Lola Bay songs. By the time I saw Dana, I was simmering with anger because of the Greek festival. I was in a mood between crying and locker kicking.

Dana read it on my face. "What?"

I kept walking. "There's a Greek festival the weekend of the concert."

"So?"

We pushed through the crowd toward my locker. "So, my dad wants the whole family to go, and no, I didn't say anything about them taking us to the concert." The custodians must have waxed the floors the night before, because the hallways were slick and had that weird smell. "My dad got tickets, and my mom has to get ready for their trip the next weekend, and my grandma is coming to stay. They filled up the whole weekend." I started to get a little choked up. I took a deep breath.

Dana ran her fingertips along the lockers as she walked. "Calm down. It's okay."

"What do you mean it's okay? I have to go to the ridiculous Greek festival."

"Maybe they'll be so busy they won't even miss you."

"Duh. I think they'd know if I wasn't there."

"I know that. I mean, by that time, it will all be worked out. They'll have so much to do, and you'll be with me and my dad, and they'll know you'll be having fun, so it will all be fine."

We reached the hallway where I had to go one way and she had to go the other.

"Your dad said yes?!"

"Not yet, but I think he will. I'm waiting until it's

closer to the concert. He's better with last-minute stuff. And if he says yes, I don't want my mom to have too much time to try to talk him out of it." She looked down at the floor.

I sighed. "If it helps, there was $10 more in the bucket this morning."

"We'll get it all. Don't worry!" She smiled and walked away.

I turned the other way and slammed right into Melanie Fish Face and the Imitators in their Lola Bay T-shirts and tattoos.

"Ewwww. Unofficial Alert," Melanie said with a scrunched-up expression. The whole group moved around me like I was poison.

I felt an arm link through mine. It was Leeza's. She pulled me along. "Ewwww. Tattooed People Alert."

The warmth of her arm felt like the old days.

When Melanie and her gang were gone, Leeza waved and hurried away, saying, "Bah!"

Bah must have been her new word. I guessed it meant *bye*, but I wondered if it meant anything else.

That night, when I should have been in bed, I stared at the bucket. We now had a total of $385, and there were fifteen days until the concert. That was plenty of time for people to donate the rest of the money. Wasn't it? I hoped it was. I put my head down on my folded arms on the desk.

I would hate it if Melanie Fish Face and her crowd all went there on the bus with chaperones, music playing, wearing their T-shirts and tattoos, and waving their light sticks at just the right time and I wasn't there. And I was Lola Bay's biggest fan. I hated that Melanie Fish Face stole the club from me. I was so mad at myself for not writing for the official club stuff. And I was so mad I didn't have real makeup for the Lola Bay Lyrics Game. I bet they would play on the bus.

We just had to get enough donations. We just had to. Come on, rainbows.

I crawled into bed and pulled my worn rosebud comforter up to my chin. My head hurt. I thought about Dana sleeping in her bed with her posters over it. Maybe her dad would say he'd take us. He was probably at his studio making art right now and humming Lola Bay songs.

I thought about Leeza and how she'd rescued me from the tattooed monsters today. I missed her, kind of.

The second I woke up on Saturday morning, I opened the computer and checked the bucket. YAY! We were at $400.

At breakfast I hummed "My Heart Soars."

"Well, who's this having such a nice morning?" said Mom.

"What?"

"You seem in a good mood, that's all."

"I guess so."

I buttered toast for myself and for the twins and cut theirs in triangles like they liked. "Dad, do you want toast?"

He looked up from his scrambled eggs. "Sure, Iris. I'll have another piece. Thanks."

In the history of me, I couldn't remember feeling this upbeat. Even though it was Saturday, I wished I could go to school and see Dana. But instead the day dragged on with me constantly checking the golden bucket.

My room seemed quieter and darker than usual that night. Mom and Dad had both knocked and said good night. I'd checked the bucket over and over, but it only had $15 more, for a total of $415.

I started worrying. This was too slow. There was no way we were going to Chicago to the concert unless we got a lot more donations—soon.

I shivered and scrunched deeper into the comfort of the bed. Outside, branches were bouncing in the wind, their tips scratching the window. The streetlight glowed through them and made them look like starving blackbirds clawing to get in from the cold. The thought crossed my mind that I should tell Robert about this. He might want to draw them.

Would Dana's dad bring the mandolin with him to Chicago? Musicians did that—carried their instruments around with them. Maybe someone in Lola Bay's band would recognize him and tell Lola Bay and she would ask him to come up onstage and play with them. And then Dana and I would get invited to go onstage with them and sing a song.

Thinking about meeting Lola Bay gave me goose bumps all up and down my arms. What would I even say to her? *I think you're incredible and talented and a great musician and I know all your songs.* I kicked the blankets with my feet. "Come on, golden bucket!" I whispered over and over.

I listened to "Nothing Is Why," and when she sang "You can't mess me up, you are nothing. Nothing is why," I felt calmer.

Sunday was more of the same. Pacing and checking. Pacing and checking. Interrupted only by taking Ian and Echo to the park and helping make Halloween costumes for them for day care. Echo wanted to be a butterfly, and Ian wanted to be a frog, then Echo wanted to be a frog too.

✦✦✦

When I got to the corner on Monday morning, Leeza nodded at me and kept her nose in her phone. "Rah."

We climbed on the bus and shuffled our way back to our seat.

"I think Robert likes you," she said, her eyes still on her phone.

I looked up from mine. "Stop it."

"No, really, Ted told me last night that he thinks so too."

I rolled my eyes. "Don't talk about me, okay?" The idea of Leeza and Ted Eckles talking about me and Robert made my eyeballs hurt.

Leeza looked sideways at me. She knew I didn't want to hear about this. "I told Ted that I didn't think you would care."

"You're right, I don't care."

"He's nice, though. Don't you think?"

"I like his birds."

Leeza looked back down. "Oh, do you want to come to another practice tonight? We can go for pizza again."

"No. I can't. Sorry." I added, "It was fun, though."

"Lola Bay stuff?" Leeza said, and rolled her eyes.

I must have sucked cold air in too fast, because I choked on my own spit.

Leeza jerked up straight like she might need to give me the Heimlich maneuver. "Are you okay?"

"I . . ." *Cough, cough.* "I breathed down air the wrong way." *Cough, cough.* "Or swallowed funny."

She looked sheepish. "Forget it. That was . . . Never mind."

Was Leeza making fun of me about Lola Bay? My nose burned as I tried to hold back tears. She was treating me like a little kid with a fangirl crush instead of someone who appreciated her music—the sound, the words, her influences. I thought she still loved Lola Bay too. Maybe not.

I stuck my nose in my phone, searching manga sites: rock star manga, manga girl with kilt, manga girl with cap on backward, manga girl with stars for eyes, neon eyes, sloppy socks, cat's ears. Anything not to look at Leeza.

When the bus stopped in front of the school, I bolted off, nearly running straight into Melanie Fish Face and the Imitators, knocking Melanie's backpack to the ground.

"Oh my gawd!" she screamed. "Watch where you walk, you klutz!" She picked up her backpack with two fingers like it had germs. "Seriously, Iris. You may owe me a new backpack."

The Imitators all nodded in unison.

All my ire got stirred up. "Forget it, Fish Face."

"What did you call me?"

I walked away. Dana was waiting for me inside the main door.

Her eyes got big as I got closer. "What was that?"

I kept walking and said, "Nothing."

I expected her to say *It didn't look like nothing*, but she didn't. She just shrugged and walked alongside me. When we reached the corner where we had to go our separate ways, she looked like she was about to say something, but I jumped in and snapped, "What?"

She stiffened all over. "What? What's your problem?"

"Nothing. I thought you were going to say something. That's all."

"I was. I was going to say I have a fantabulous idea to tweak Melanie Fish Face."

She suddenly had my attention. "What?" I wanted to hear it.

"Well, to start, we have to be in the same place as her when she's using her phone."

She must have seen my brows knit as I tried to think what this might be.

"Stop worrying. It's nothing we could get caught at. And it's hilarious."

"Hilarious? Really? What is it?"

"Trust me. You have to see it to appreciate it. We just have to be in the same place as them where there is Wi-Fi."

I didn't mean to agree to whatever it was, but a light bulb went off in my head. "They were at Pizza Papa's when I went last time."

"That would be perfect."

"Maybe they'll be there tonight." I thought about Leeza and her gang being there and wondered if Dana and I could go along, and we just wouldn't talk to them much. "Leeza and some kids from her team will be there. We could sit with them. Hide in a group."

Dana looked like she was going to say *no way* to sitting with Leeza and her friends. Then she tilted her head and said, "Good idea. We could do what we need to do from a crowded table of kids."

That left me with the problem of asking Leeza if I could bring Dana to her pizza party after I'd said I couldn't go.

I caught Leeza in the hallway outside the library.

"Hey!"

"Rah. 'Sup?"

"Are you still going to Pizza Papa's tonight?"

"Yes. I told you on the bus."

"Can Dana and I come?"

Leeza stopped. Behind her eyes I could see an *ugh*. But good ol' Leeza rallied and said, "Does she really want to hang out with a bunch of sixth graders?"

"She hangs out with me."

"Yeah, but this would be, like, in public."

I paused.

She paused.

Then we both laughed at the idea of Dana at a table of sixth graders at Pizza Papa's.

"Okay. I'll see if she really wants to," I said. "I thought the pizza was good, that's all. Do Melanie Fisher and her friends always come to Pizza Papa's?"

"OMG, yes. They are so annoying."

I nodded.

As she walked away, she said over her shoulder, "The pizza's not that good, but she's welcome anyway. And you don't have to tell me why you want to go. Yes, Robert will be there."

She waved her hand to stop me. "Oh, and it's Halloween, so wear a mask."

✦ ✦ ✦

Even though it was Halloween—which I can't believe I forgot—and I'd told Mom I would go with her and the twins to a Halloween party, she happily agreed I could go with Leeza to Pizza Papa's. Dana was jazzed about going, and she especially liked the idea that we'd be wearing masks. She only worried that Melanie Fish Face might not show up. I drifted by Fish Face and the Imitators in the lunchroom to see if I could overhear their plans. They all turned and stared at me until I felt like limp lettuce from the salad bar and moved on.

I suggested to Dana that we watch Leeza's volleyball practice.

"Isn't it loud and boring?"

"Yeah, but it's, like, her pizza party we're going to, so . . ."

"Fine. Don't care," she said distractedly. Her mind looked to be on whatever we were going to do when we achieved the same Wi-Fi space as Melanie Fish Face.

While we sat in the bleachers, I watched practice and Dana fiddled with my phone.

"What are you doing?" I asked her.

"I'm setting up a free VPN."

"What's a VPN?"

"It makes you untraceable online."

"Why don't you put it on your phone?"

"Duh, Wi-Fi?"

"Oh yeah, right. Are you on Wi-Fi now on my phone?"

She nodded with her nose pointed into the screen. "Uh-huh. The school guest Wi-Fi."

"But they don't know it's me?"

She pointed at me. "Exactly."

"So, what are we going to do to Melanie Fish Face?"

"Wait. It's going to be so cool."

"It's not a stealing thing, is it?" My nervousness sprang into action. "I'm not up for any more of that pay-wall stuff."

"No. Not at all. You are going to love it and thank me."

The boys across the gym nudged each other and tried not to look at us. I could tell that Dana scared them. Not only was she a seventh grader, but she wore dresses, had unusual hair, and walked tall and didn't slouch. They were louder than before and red-faced.

When the practice was over, Leeza ran toward us and waved to us to come.

"Did you bring masks?" she asked us.

Dana and I held up the masks we'd made in Studio Arts. Hers was wild modern art. Mine was a manga version of Lola Bay.

Everyone mumbled "heys," and we walked in three groups to Pizza Papa's: Leeza and Regina in front wearing matching pirate masks, the guys next, each with a different mask, and me and Dana last.

Peter Papa had decorated the place with spiderwebs and ghosts, and there were pumpkins on all the tables. We all ordered slices, then scraped chairs around a table in the corner. Melanie Fish Face was nowhere in sight. Ted carved a hole in the pumpkin on our table and the server told him to "knock it off." There wasn't much conversation after that. It was like Dana's presence had thrown a wet blanket over the pizza party.

Leeza tried. "Have you been here before, Dana?"

"Nope." She was deep in my phone.

Regina even tried. "You play any sports, Dana?"

This almost got a laugh from her. "Nope."

The boys didn't open their mouths until they could shovel pizza into them.

I kept checking the door for Melanie Fish Face and the Imitators. They didn't come and didn't come. I also kept looking at Robert's mask. I finally said, "What's your mask?"

"It's a blue eagle face."

"Wow, that's really cool."

"Thanks. I like yours too. I've seen you drawing it a lot."

"Yeah, I'm influenced by manga."

When I'd almost given up waiting for Melanie Fish Face, the door opened and a cold wind carried the Official Lola Bay Fan Club into Pizza Papa's, including Salima, Callie, Bethany, and Paige. They were all wearing sunglasses with giant jeweled cat eyes. By this time, many of the tables were occupied, and Melanie and her gang had to sit in an opposite corner of the restaurant. I felt a ripple of excitement.

Dana sat up at attention. She kept her eyes on Melanie and waited for her to take out her phone. It only took seconds. Melanie talked and scrolled and laughed and texted. On and on. Dana pressed key after key. I tried to look at my screen, but she rotated it away.

"What are you doing?" I whispered.

"Hang on," she answered.

Then, finally, she threw back her head and laughed and pumped her fist. "Yes!"

"What?!" I whispered.

"Come here." Dana scooted her chair a foot away from the table and motioned to me to do the same.

I leaned over and couldn't understand what I was looking at on my screen.

"What is it?"

"Just look. Read it."

I focused and realized I was looking at a text. Not one of mine—Melanie Fisher's texts! I pushed Dana's arm. "How did you do that?"

"Easy. Her password is—guess what that nutball's password is."

"I don't know. Maybe *Lola Bay* or something like that."

"Close. Fish Face uses the password *LolaBayOfficial1*."

"How did you do it?"

"With the VPN, and I guessed the password. Easy."

We were now deep in our own conversation, and the rest of our group started talking among themselves. Little nervous bubbles formed in my stomach. "Are you sure it can't be traced to my phone?"

"Calm down. I'm sure."

"What are you going to do?"

"What do you think? We can send texts from her account to anyone—like we are *her*. Who do we want her to text, and what should it say?"

My slight feelings of this being wrong were completely overwhelmed by the fun of it. "I suppose we could have her send a text to a boy."

"Uh-huh, but that's kind of boring," said Dana.

"Oh, okay. I guess so."

She rubbed her hands together like she was cooking up something. "We could send one to one of the Imitators saying something bad about another one, and then blind copy that other one."

I thought about that for a second, then gasped. "OMG! That's really funny." The heads at our table turned to me for a second, then went back to their own business. "Let's do it. Send one to Vivian saying something snarky about Zoe. Then copy Zoe."

"Like what? What do you think they care about?"

"Say Zoe's hair is ugly and she never should have cut it or something. I don't know. Something like that."

It took only seconds. Dana started typing.

> Z's hair is ugly. She never should have cut it. Too bad it will be that way for the concert.

She pressed Send. We watched from across the room as Vivian read it and looked at Zoe. In a split second she keyed a reply.

> Totally ugly.

Immediately, both Fish Face and Zoe looked at their phones. Fish Face looked confused. Zoe went pale. She jumped up and threw her slice of pizza, cheesy side down, onto Melanie's lap and screamed, "You told me to cut my hair!"

Fish Face jumped up and screamed, sending drinks spilling all over the table, but not before Zoe could grab hers and pitch it into Vivian's face.

I screamed and covered my mouth.

The squealing in that corner of Pizza Papa's drew the attention of everyone in the place, including the manager, who ran over and told them all to get out.

Fish Face, Vivian, and Zoe all left in tears. The rest of them looked bewildered, but they left the restaurant as ordered.

Leeza said, "What's their problem?"

True to form, Ted said, "Dunno."

16

NOT-NICE FEELINGS

THAT NIGHT, I thought about Zoe throwing the pizza in Fish Face's lap and the Sprite in Vivian's face. It was funny, but setting them up was really mean. It was the first really mean thing I'd ever done. It made me feel a little icky. Even if Melanie had been awful to us, and she deserved her share of awfulness back, it didn't feel good to be the one doing it.

Then I wondered again if there was any way that they could trace the text to my phone. Dana swore there was none. I figured if she was smart enough to do it, she was probably smart enough to cover her tracks.

In the morning, I was eager to see Dana. I wanted to

tell her that I thought that was enough punking Melanie Fish Face, and when I said I didn't want to break through any more walls, I meant phone walls too.

I was so amped up, I almost forgot to check the golden bucket. I ran back to find it had $510!

On the bus, I was almost giggly.

"What's up?" Leeza asked.

"Nothing," I said with a sly smile.

When I got off the bus, Dana was waiting. She raised her hand for a high five and I slapped it.

"Wait until you see them. They're twisted up in knots!"

I scrunched my shoulders and laughed into my hand. "Okay, but I don't want to do that again, it was too scary. What if they find out?"

I didn't have to wait long to see the effect of our punk. We turned the corner by the office, and Fish Face, Vivian, and Zoe were arguing in the doorway. The rest of the Imitators were across the hall, giving them some space.

"Zoe, I never said that!" Melanie insisted.

Zoe shook her phone in front of Melanie's eyes. "You said it in a text to Vivian. Right here!"

Vivian looked cornered. "I did get the text."

Zoe waved the phone in Vivian's face. "And you agreed!"

Melanie rolled her eyes so hard, her bangs fluffed. "If

I were going to say something mean about you, why in the world would I copy you on the text?"

"You copied me by mistake, that's why. And you got caught!" said Zoe, still waving her phone around.

Melanie pushed past Zoe. "I'm tired of this. I refuse to talk about it anymore. I didn't send the text and that's that. Don't you get it? Someone is punking me. I don't know how, but I'll find out. So, enough, Zoe. Okay?"

Dana and I backed up against the lockers as they fumed by.

"Let's get out of here." She pulled me away.

I went through the rest of the morning enjoying the image of Melanie getting yelled at.

Everywhere I went, kids were talking about trouble in Fisher-land.

When I got to Studio Arts, Dana gave me a grin and a thumbs-up. I laughed, but then I thought about the possibility of Fish Face figuring out it was from my phone, and my stomach churned.

I grabbed a black charcoal stick and started drawing a manga Lola Bay. The arching circles of the eyes, the scratching of the charcoal on the paper made my shoulders relax.

Ms. Wells paused by me. I heard her take a breath to speak, but then she must have seen me squeeze my charcoal stick, and she backed away.

I concentrated on my drawing for the whole period. Near the end I looked over at Robert Benally, and he gave me a small wave with a paintbrush wet with cadmium red. I half smiled.

I went through the motions of paying attention for the rest of the day, then climbed onto the bus like a zombie. Leeza was nose-down in her phone.

I watched as a girl five rows ahead of us put her gum into the center of the ponytail of the girl in the seat in front of her. There was no stopping it. The girl felt something and turned around. When she realized what had happened, she screamed, "Ariel, you're horrible. I'm telling on you. You wait."

The girl with the gummed hair cried. Her friend reached to take the gum out, and the girl slapped her hand. "Leave it, Mia."

Ariel smiled and laughed with the girl next to her.

Okay, that was mean. Ariel was squarely a not-nice girl. Anyone could tell that.

I sort of wished for an "undo" of the text prank.

The bus rumbled along with mean things happening in the seats all around me. I tried to force my brain to focus on the concert. As I watched Lola Bay on YouTube, I thought about how much fun we were going to have in Chicago. I imagined being in the crowd outside the door, with all the free stuff Dana had ordered. Finding our seats and getting a program, and how the air would be electric. The lights would go dark and then they'd flash and Lola Bay would be singing live!

We had eleven days to get the rest of the money. I hummed "Blamed and Broken" and went back to dreaming about feeling the pounding of the drums and bass guitar in my blood. Then suddenly the bus driver was yelling. "Girls, your stop!" Leeza shouldered me out of my daze.

I climbed off the bus and headed toward my house, stopping for a few seconds to take a closer look at the bittersweet in Mr. Reynolds's yard. I thought about a new painting with the sumac bush leaves next to it.

When I looked up, Dana was in front of my house.

She said, "Hey, let's go check the bucket."

"Okay," I said, relieved.

She stashed her bike in the same old place by the side of the porch and followed me in.

"Want a snack?" I asked her.

"No."

"We have crackers and peanut butter."

She laughed. "Then no for sure."

"Right." I grabbed a couple tangerines and some Ritz crackers. "Come on."

Dana went straight to my computer and turned it on. As soon as it came to life, she clicked into the site and jumped up, knocking the chair over. "Squeaking armadillos! We're at $650!"

I rushed to the desk. The donations were all small ones, but they were coming in: $5 and $10 donations. And the last one, $10, was from Ms. Wells. "Look! Ms. Wells gave us $10."

"We're almost there!!!!" Dana said. "We only need $750 plus $300, or $1050, to make it. We'll get that. I'm so sure."

"Oh my gosh. This is great."

"And if we get more than we need, we can buy some stuff in Chicago. Some cool souvenirs or something."

"How will we do that?" I asked. "We said we could only use the card for the tickets."

Dana rolled her eyes. "How exactly do you think all the donation money is going to pay for things?"

I didn't know. I hadn't thought about it.

She knocked on my head with her fist and I ducked away. "Dodo. We only spend what's ours. We leave the ticket money in the account and use the card for the bus, the hotel, the restaurants, and whatever . . . up to the total that's ours. No problem."

The logic of it was there in plain sight. I remembered

that she had that little slip of paper with the credit card number on it. She was right. There was no reason we couldn't spend what was ours. "Don't do it without telling me, though. I have to say it's okay, because it's my family's card."

Dana took her hands off the keyboard and let them rest in her lap.

I waited for her to say *Okay*, but she didn't. She just looked at her hands.

I wasn't sure what was going to happen next.

Finally, she said, "Whatever you say, Iris. It's your computer, your funding page, your golden bucket, your family's credit card." She took a deep breath and let it out slowly. "It's all yours."

"Stop it. It is not. It's ours."

A knock on the door startled us. Mom popped her head in. From the look on her face, we startled her too.

"Oh, hello, Dana. Iris, I just wanted to let you know we're home." She pulled back and started to shut the door.

"Hello, Mrs. Underwood," Dana said. She smiled bigger than I'd ever seen her smile. It was like she'd overheard what Mom had said about her.

Mom smiled back at her with a surprised expression.

"Do you need help with snacks for the twins?" I asked.

"No, that's okay, Iris."

"Really, I'll help." I wasn't sure why I was offering to do this, but something pulled me up out of my chair toward the door. I said to Dana, "I'll be right back."

"Sure. I'm just going to do some homework." But her head was in screen-land.

17

THE CONTEST!

BY FRIDAY, EIGHT days before the concert, we had $720, and I was convinced we were going to get there. Dana was acting silly—almost giddy. When we got off the bus and were walking to my house, I said, "Have you asked your dad yet?"

"I'm waiting for the perfect time. I'm pretty sure he's going to say yes. He's been in a really good mood lately."

"Good, because I'm going to have to tell my parents soon."

"Don't worry, Iris. This is all going to work out. I can feel it. Your parents won't have to do anything but say okay. Trust me. You trust me, don't you?"

"Sure," I said.

"I can trust you, can't I?" she pressed me.

"Sure. What do you mean?" I wasn't sure what I was being trusted for.

"You know how I did that thing on the computer in the library and with Fish Face's phone? You wouldn't tell on me, would you?"

I bugged my eyes, like, *No*. That was water under the bridge, like Dad said about things that were done and couldn't be changed. "But let's not do it anymore. It makes me too nervous."

We walked along in silence, and then Dana said almost under her breath, "I was thinking, on the Friday night before the concert, you could stay over at my house."

I stopped. "Really? You want me to come to your house for an overnight?"

"Sure. You can be with us the whole weekend that way."

I felt a happy hum inside as we ran into my house and up to the computer to see how much we had in the bucket.

My friendship feelings were interrupted by an alert message on my laptop, in a text and email, announcing a contest.

"What is it?" Dana asked.

The message was from a local radio station, with the

subject line "Lola Bay—*Stars in Cars* in Minnesota."

We crowded in so closely to the computer, our heads touched. I opened the email.

LOLA BAY ★ *STARS IN CARS* CONTEST ★ MINNESOTA ★ KDQB

SURPRISE! Your favorite radio station KDQB is offering a pop-up contest for one lucky LOLA BAY fan to ride with her in a special episode of *Stars in Cars* on the morning of November 12, the last day of Lola Bay's tour. The event will be filmed and broadcast live at the Minneapolis Target Center. Entrants must be at least 12 years old (with parental or guardian approval under 18), and the winner (and parent or guardian) must sign required waivers and releases. Enter by clicking the link below and filling out the attached form no later than midnight, November 6. The winner will be selected November 9. The lucky winner must be in Minneapolis on November 12 and ready to ride.

We stared at each other. Was this real? Lola Bay was coming to Minneapolis and was going to do *Stars in Cars* with a fan on the morning of the last concert?

We had to enter. Had to!

Dana shoved the laptop my way.

My hands were shaking as I clicked the link.

An entry form appeared asking for my name, address, age, email, and favorite Lola Bay songs. Then I had to fill in the blank: "Why do you love LOLA BAY songs?" I filled in everything until I had to come up with the reason.

"You could say they changed your life," Dana offered.

"No," I said, waving that idea away. "Let me think."

"How about—"

"Stop," I interrupted her. "I'll do mine and you do your own. I need to think."

"Fine," she said, and she took out one of my manga books and pretended to read. "Let me know when you're done." She yawned like she expected it to be forever.

Suddenly, I knew my answer. I keyed in:

> Lola Bay's songs find the little hurt in my heart and mend it.

Before Dana could sit up and look at it, I hit Enter.

Next, I had to print the form and get one of my parents to sign on the bottom, then scan it and send it back to the link indicated.

"How do I scan it?" I wondered out loud.

"Give me your phone," Dana ordered.

I gave her a sharp look. "No. Wait. Don't break any walls."

"I won't, dodo. I'll download a free scanner app while you're getting it signed."

"Oh, okay."

I grabbed the form and raced to find one of my parents. I found Dad at his desk in the spare room.

"Dad!" I burst into the room.

"What's the matter, Iris? Is something wrong?" He pushed back his chair like I'd scared him.

"Nothing's wrong. I just need you to sign this form."

He reached for it. "Is it for school?"

"No, it's for riding in *Stars in Cars* with Lola Bay."

"What?"

"It's a contest to be picked to be on the *Stars in Cars* program and ride with Lola Bay."

He smiled and picked up his pen. "Oh, I know that show. It's fun. With the camera looking in the front seat and the star and passenger singing. I liked that one with what's-her-name."

"Yeah, that's it."

"They don't really drive the car, do they?"

"I don't know. All I know is that to enter, I need you to sign. And if I win, there's a bunch of waivers and releases and stuff." I don't know why I was so impatient. It didn't say the entries were being judged on how fast they got in. I just wanted mine in right away.

"I suppose there will be quite a few entries," he said as he looked it over.

"Yeah, I think like a million, for sure."

"Oh, wait one minute, Iris."

My heart stopped. "What?"

"This is November twelfth. That's the day of the Greek festival."

I thought my brain was going to explode. I slumped against the doorframe. "DAD!"

"What's going on?" Mom was now on the scene.

He held up the paper. "Iris wants to enter a contest with a million other kids to be on *Stars in Cars* with Lola Bay on the same day as the Greek festival."

"Is this what you were so upset about the other day?" she asked.

"Oh my gosh! Can't I enter a contest? It's, like, here in Minneapolis. This will never happen again."

"I don't know, Marnie. If she wins, I guess we'll all have to go, and the twins will miss their dynamite souvlaki."

Suddenly, I caught the tone in his voice, and I could tell he was teasing me. My shoulders dropped from up by my ears. "That's not funny."

Mom put her hand over her smile. "I think if Iris wins a contest with a million entries, we'll work it out."

Dad moved his pen in a big circle with a fancy swirl and made a big deal of signing the form.

I grabbed it. "Thanks!"

When I got back upstairs, Dana was waiting with the phone app.

"Lay it on the desk," she said, pointing.

She took a picture of it and sent the file to my email. Next, on the laptop, she went to the box for submitting the form and uploaded it. She clicked Send, and it was done. I received an email almost instantly telling me my entry had been received.

"Now you enter," I said.

"I don't have a computer to enter from."

"Use mine."

"I need a parental signature."

"Your dad will sign, won't he?"

She turned the keyboard toward me. "Check the bucket."

"Dana?"

"I'll ask him when I get home and he wakes up. He probably will. No sweat."

I quickly found the bucket, and it had $895.

We both squealed and jumped up and down.

◆◆◆

Monday marked the real countdown—six days to go. Dana wiggled her eyebrows at me from behind her easel in Studio Arts. I sent her back silly looks.

"Today, everyone will try a mixed-media collage." Ms. Wells strolled around the room. "Bottles of ink and paper palettes with acrylics are on the counter. There's a box of paper and fabric scraps here in the center of the room."

She paused at my easel. "You always do manga of Lola Bay. Why not try to zero in on one part of her and do a closer study? Just an idea."

I tilted my head, looked at the canvas, and thought about Lola's eyes.

Ms. Wells moved on to Jess Soderberg, who could never figure out what to do, and said, "Get that stack of *New York Times Book Review*s and bring them over here."

I lined up a row of Lola cutouts and stared at them. The bodies were dressed in the black tee with lots of bracelets. The lips pouted pink, or red, or in a kiss shape. I looked in the eyes and saw something I had never noticed before. She looked like a little kid dressed up like an adult for Halloween. They all signaled nervousness. I couldn't believe it. She'd been looking out at the world from magazine pages for months, saying it was scary and hard.

When the bell rang, Dana ducked out the door. I hurried after her. She grabbed my arm and pulled me into the computer lab, to a spot where the screen was private.

We flopped down and she started clicking like crazy, pulling up pages and moving through them. I assumed she was looking for our bucket, but she landed on the Blue Sky Airlines home page.

"How exactly are you doing this? I thought we couldn't surf the whole web here."

"It's simple. I guessed the administrator's password."

"You guessed it?"

"No, not exactly guessed it. If you go behind the teacher's counter at the front up there, it's written on a sticky." She pointed to the screen. "Look, round-trip airfare is $317 each plus tax."

"We don't have that much money," I said.

"I know it's more, but we may need to fly."

"Why?"

"Well, if you win *Stars in Cars*, you can't be on a bus at the same time you're singing in a car with Lola Bay in downtown Minneapolis."

Yikes. I didn't think about that. She was right. The bus left in the morning. *Stars in Cars* was in the morning. "What do you think the chances are that I'll win *Stars in Cars*?"

"It depends on how many people enter."

"Do you think it will be a million?"

"It will be a lot, for sure."

"Did you enter?"

She hesitated, then smiled. "No. I wanted you to have a better chance."

"Aw. That's so nice." The idea warmed my heart. "Hey, let's look at the bucket."

"Okay, let's look."

She pulled up our page. It said $970.

"What!" we yelped, and everyone turned to look at us.

"Shush, be quiet."

"Oh my gosh! Who is giving us all this money?" I said. "Look at the individual donations."

"They're all small, I think." She tapped her hand on the table. "So, should we buy plane tickets?"

"Have you asked your dad?"

"Not yet, but I'm pretty sure he will do it. He loves concerts."

"I don't think we should buy any tickets of any kind until we have all the money in the bucket."

Dana pounded the table with her fist like she was going to argue, but then she relaxed. "Fine. We'll have to think of a way to get those contributions coming in faster, that's all."

"Do you think I'll win *Stars in Cars*? Really?"

She looked at me. "You never know. Think hard that you will. Now you have to go catch your bus. I'll see you later." She shooed me away.

She came over that night and brought the box from the Lola Bay Fan Club with everything we'd asked for. It felt like Christmas, Hanukkah, Kwanza, and all the holidays rolled into one. The box was packed with stick faces, bracelets, light sticks, PopSockets, tattoos—everything Melanie Fish Face and the Imitators had and more. We sang in the mirror. Mom came up and told us to keep it down.

Finally, Dana sat down at my computer while I did my homework.

"You're not breaking into any walls, are you?" I asked her.

"Nope."

"What's all that weird stuff going by in blocks?"

"It's code, that's all. Relax. I'm just exercising my brain."

I finally relaxed and concentrated on good thoughts like winning the contest. I kept coming up with better answers, but it was too late. I crossed my fingers for the one I'd sent. There was not much to do now but watch the bucket and wait for the results of the contest.

By the time she was ready to go home, we had $1030.

"Tomorrow we'll buy the plane tickets, right?" she said.

"Okay," I finally agreed. We high-fived. "Ask your dad tonight, promise," I pressed her.

"I will."

18

TEXT OF A LIFETIME

I KEPT IMAGINING Dana in the kitchen with her dad. He would be playing his mandolin and be in a super-good mood, and she would make mint tea and he would say, "Hey, how was school?" and she would say, "Really good. Guess what? Lola Bay has added concert dates in Chicago this weekend," and he would stop strumming and say, "Wow! We should go," and she would say, "Really! Can Iris come with us?" and he would say, "Sure." Sometimes in my daydream, I had Mr. Dean say, "Why don't you ask your friend Iris," and she would say, "Thanks. That's a great idea."

This daydream gave me so much hope, but it was nothing like the reality that happened on Wednesday at

4:38 p.m., when I got the text that changed my life. When my phone dinged, I pulled it out of my pocket and read. My mouth started moving, but nothing came out. I read it again and again.

Congratulations Iris Underwood. This is KDQB. You are the lucky winner of the Stars in Cars contest. Please contact John Barnes at 612 233 5555 immediately. Have a parent or guardian available to discuss details. Your submission was selected by Lola Bay herself!

Then I screamed, "Mom!"

She was in the kitchen trying to get dinner together when I fell through the doorway.

"I won the *Stars in Cars* contest!"

I stood there in a daze. Was this really happening? "Did you hear me? I won *Stars in Cars*!"

"Good for you. Can you set the table?"

"You're not listening!" I jumped around the kitchen. "*Stars in Cars*, Mom. *Stars in Cars*."

"Of course I'm listening. Can you set the table, please?"

"No, you're not!" I put my phone screen in front of her face. "Read this!"

She leaned back like I'd put it too close for her

to see it. I watched her lips move silently as she read through the text. Then suddenly she understood. Her face changed from stressed to a big smile. "This is that thing! You won that thing!"

"Yes. I won that thing, and we have to call John Barnes. The radio station wants us to call John Barnes. Me and a parent or guardian. Right away."

"Let me look at that again after dinner. Right now, set the table, please, Miss Star-in-the-Car."

The door opened and Dad walked in.

I screamed, "Dad! I won *Stars in Cars*!" and hopped across the kitchen like I was on a pogo stick.

"Wow. Iris. Wait—you won? I thought there were a million entries." He made a *pfft* sound. "Unbelievable!"

I jumped up and down and waved my arms. "I won *Stars in Cars*!"

"Iris, calm down. Let's get through dinner and we'll talk about it."

My phone vibrated again. This time it was an email saying the same thing as the text. The pressure to reply was enormous. So I did.

> Got your text and email. YAY!
> V-excited. My parents will call you
> soon. YAY!!!!!!!!

I read it and added more exclamation points. *!!!!!!* And pressed Send.

I read the texts and the email so many times, I could recite them by heart. I also located my form and read my winning entry over and over. *Lola Bay's songs find the little hurt in my heart and mend it.*

FINALLY, at 5:55 p.m., mostly because I didn't eat a thing and I hurried Ian and Echo with every bite, dinner was over. I was worried sick that John Barnes would go to the second-place winner if he didn't get my forms. Mom and Dad sat at the kitchen table looking at the email that I'd printed.

"What do you think, Marnie?"

"What do you think, Charles?"

My heart was about to explode. What was there to think?

Dad sat back. "I don't know. What about the Greek festival?"

I screamed, "Dad!!!!"

He laughed. Mom laughed. I didn't think it was funny.

"It's impressive," Mom continued, "that they selected your statement about the music."

"I was impressed by what you wrote," Dad added.

Yes! "So let's call, okay?" I handed over my phone. "Let's call the radio station, get the releases and waivers, so they know I'm coming."

FINALLY, we called John Barnes at the radio station and my parents asked him all kinds of questions about the car—which actually doesn't drive—and he emailed them the waivers and releases.

He was friendly and fast talking like a voice on the air. "Once we get them back from you, it will be a go. Tomorrow morning we'll make the announcement that Iris is the winner. You should expect some press contacts. Just say how excited you are. That's all you need to do. You'll be contacted by Lola Bay's advance person, and we'll send you all the details for where to meet on Saturday morning."

I bit my knuckle to keep from shrieking with joy.

"Thanks very much, John," Dad said. "This will be an experience for our girl."

"You might like to know that the team at the station reviewed the five thousand or so entries and narrowed them down to ten and sent them to Lola Bay. She picked the one Iris sent in."

Mom smiled. "We thought it was great too."

"Five thousand, you say?" asked Dad. "I thought you'd have a million." He winked at me.

"Oh no. That's why we announced with such a short window. You wouldn't believe it. Forty-five hundred of them were, like, 'wows me, great vibes, cool tunes,' stuff like that. We really only had about five hundred who made a meaningful effort."

I wanted so much to tell Dana, but I figured it would be more fun when I saw her in person and I had the official announcement.

✦ ✦ ✦

The next morning, I looked all over for Dana but didn't see her until Studio Arts. I grabbed her and yelled, "I won *Stars in Cars*!!!!"

She jumped around with me, and all the kids around us wanted to know what was going on. I told them I had won the *Stars in Cars* contest and I was going to sing in a car with Lola Bay on Saturday morning.

Ms. Wells stopped by my easel and winked at me. "Congratulations on the *Stars in Cars* thing, Iris." Then she put something the size of a brick in my backpack on the floor. "I'm so happy for you at a time like this. This is for your family."

I smiled at her and said, "Thanks." It didn't take long to figure out by the aroma that it was banana bread. Weird that she gave me that.

Dana darted out of the room at the end of class. I thought she would want to come over and celebrate and plan going downtown Saturday morning, but she was gone. In all the excitement, I forgot to ask her if her dad had said he would take us to Chicago.

On the bus, Leeza said, "Wow. That's so lucky to happen right now and all. I'm really happy for you. Regina and Ted and I are going to come to the Target Center and watch you." When we got off the bus and were about to head to our separate houses, she gave me a huge, tight hug.

"Thanks," I said. I guessed people liked you more when you were a little famous.

When I got to our house, there was a huge box on our front porch. It was too big for me to move, so I squished past it to the door.

Inside, Mom was making snacks. I handed her the aluminum-foil-wrapped brick. "This is from Ms. Wells for the family."

"Oh, that's nice. What is it?" she asked.

"It smells like banana bread," I said.

She laughed. She unwrapped it and took a sniff. "How nice of her. You'll have to say thank you."

As I headed for the stairs, I yelled, "I did. Oh, there's a big box on the front porch."

"What?" she yelled back.

"A BIG BOX ON THE FRONT PORCH," I yelled.

I heard her open the front door. "What on earth?"

This caught my attention, and I pivoted to go back down. "What is it?"

"It's a giant box of diapers." She was dragging it in by

one open flap. She looked it over for some sign of who it was from but couldn't find a name. "I suppose your father ordered these." She sighed.

"I have homework," I said, not wanting to get involved in the diaper mystery.

I pounded up the stairs and banged my door open with my backpack. It slipped to the floor as I opened my computer and clicked straight to the golden bucket.

Sixteen hundred dollars! What?! I started calculating the difference between bus tickets and airline tickets.

The doorbell rang, interrupting my math.

Mom yelled from downstairs. "IRIS, CAN YOU GET THAT? I'VE GOT MY HANDS FULL."

I groaned and tore my eyes away from the bucket. Just as I moved, I heard a jingle. Another $25! It must just take some time for people to find you on this site. I imagined that one person saw it and told their friends, and they told their friends, and they told their friends. How brilliant was this!

I clomped down to the front door, expecting to see the UPS man, but no one was there. If I hadn't smelled something, I would have missed it. There was a casserole on the porch! What the heck? I reached down to pick it up, and it was warm. A sticky note on the side said, "30 minutes at 350."

I carried it into the kitchen by its two handles. "This was on the porch. It says thirty minutes at three fifty."

Mom paused from wiping Echo's hands. "What on earth?" She lifted the lid. "Smells like a tuna noodle casserole."

I looked over her shoulder and saw crumbled potato chips on top. "Who's it from?"

She looked it all over. "I don't know. Was there a card with it?"

"I didn't see one."

Mom took off to the front door like she didn't believe me. After a long search around the porch, she came back in. "Nope. Nothing. Why would someone leave us a casserole? I wonder if it's at the wrong house."

"Maybe it's because I won *Stars in Cars*?" I was getting used to being famous.

She looked at me like, *I don't think so.*

The garage door rolled up, telling us that Dad was home—early. He opened the door and looked around. "Anything funny going on around here?"

Mom laughed. "You mean other than that you ordered a million diapers, and someone left a tuna casserole on the front porch? No. Nothing unusual."

He took off his coat and started to clean the graham crackers off Ian. "I got a few crazy texts and emails today. And some of the other professors were giving me sad smiles or thumbs-up."

I sat down at the table. "Was it about *Stars in Cars*?"

"I don't think so, Iris. Not everything is about you," Dad said, and squeezed my shoulder.

"Well, what did they say?" Mom asked.

He pulled his phone out of his pocket. "Listen to this: *Buck up, old boy.* And *Tough shakes.* And *I might know about an opening teaching online.*" He looked back and forth at us. "What do you think? Has the world gone mad? Or is something bad about to happen to my job?"

Mom's face sobered. "Did your dean say anything?"

Dad shook his head. "No. I checked my trash and my spam folders. I didn't get laid off by email or text today." He made a clueless face. "I have no idea."

Mom dropped onto a kitchen chair with a damp dish towel limp in her hand. "I wonder if that's why we got the casserole . . . and the diapers."

"What's that about diapers?" Dad asked. "The twins are almost done with them."

Mom weakly waved the towel toward the dining room and Dad walked over.

"Wow. That's a big box of diapers!" He laughed.

Mom looked like she was going to cry. "Obviously,

someone thinks you've lost your job . . . or you're going to lose it."

Dad rubbed the back of his neck like it was stiff.

Mom looked at him with a grave expression. "Do you think you should call Dean Frasier and find out what's going on?"

"I'm not sure I want to know." Dad worked harder on his neck. "Oh, this is silly. It must be some kind of mistake. I'll get it cleared up tomorrow."

I thought about saying, *Maybe the diapers are a gift because I won* Stars in Cars, but they weren't in the mood.

After dinner I went upstairs to do my homework. Of course, I checked the bucket.

WHAM! I about fell off my chair when I saw the amount: $3,995! This was nuts. I checked the individual donations. They were all anonymous. The whole time I was on the site, the bell kept dinging. Shimmers and coins kept flowing. I finally shut it off when it hit $5,025. I was exhausted from the adrenaline rush of watching each donation drop in.

I crawled into bed and pulled the covers up to my chin. Who would have guessed that the internet was so powerful that all those people would find their way to my little page with its little wish to go to Chicago and give me so much money? Then I realized, duh! People must have heard that I won *Stars in Cars* and looked me up on the internet and found the site and thought, *This girl won* Stars in Cars. *She deserves to go to the concert in Chicago!*

A soft knock at the door was followed by Mom popping her head in. "Don't you worry about any of this."

"What?"

She smiled. "Never mind. I know where your mind is. I thought maybe you were concerned about Dad's strange business at work."

"He's not really losing his job, is he?"

"Ah, so you are paying attention. No. I'm sure he's not. He'll talk to the dean tomorrow and get it all cleared up. Good night, Iris."

"Good night, Mom."

What if Dad really was losing his job? What would we do? Could we buy food? Would we have to leave our house?

I glanced over at my computer. The golden bucket had lots of money in it that could help my family. And it would be a surprise to my parents since it would go straight to their credit card.

Maybe I'd finally done something good, even if I hadn't planned it that way. Even if half of it was technically Dana's money.

I slipped out of bed to stare at the golden bucket one more time.

Of course the internet decided to be super-slow. Wait. Wait. Wait.

WHAT? The bucket was sprouting rainbows and sending swirling spirals across the screen. It was hard to see what was going on behind all the graphics.

Then it cleared and I saw the bucket total: $20,000. The chair fell backward, and my feet flew into the air. I jumped up and pointed at the screen. The room started spinning. I threw my hands over my mouth to squelch a scream. Oh my gosh! Oh my gosh! There must be some mistake.

I clicked on "Your Public Dream Page." I hadn't actually looked at the public-facing page in a while, almost since the beginning. It popped up and I froze.

My same picture was at the top, with my same wish for money to go to the Lola Bay concert in Chicago underneath.

But there was a new paragraph. I shook my head, but it didn't go away. I sat down and reread it.

> Please help. I haven't been able to say this until now, but it's true, my dad is losing his job and our family is on the verge of being homeless, and we may have to live in our car in a parking lot.

The words ricocheted around in my head until they sank in. I waved my hands like they were hot.

DANA! Dana must have done this. I needed to get it off of there. OFF. OFF. OFF.

I shakily pressed Edit Your Profile.

It asked for my password.

Where was the password? Had Dana given me the password? I had seen her write it down.

I yanked my desk drawer open and scrambled through pencils, pens, markers, erasers, old birthday cards, paper clips, Lola Bay wristbands, candy wrappers.

NOTHING. NOTHING. NOTHING. It wasn't there.

I swept my hands across the top of the desk and moved books, notebooks, papers, magazines, empty paper cups. I lifted the laptop to see if she'd hidden it underneath. Nothing.

Tears came. Hot angry tears. I didn't know what to do. Should I run and tell my parents? Should I wait until tomorrow morning and shake it out of Dana?

Oh no. This must be why people were treating Dad like he'd lost his job! This was why there were diapers at the door! And tuna casserole . . . with potato chips!

I paced around my room.

Biting my knuckle.

What should I do? What should I do?

Get it down. I had to get it off there.

Calm down, Iris, I commanded myself. *Just reset the password. Reset the password, that's all. Reset the password.*

I took a deep shaky breath and sat down. The empty field waited for me.

Password: _____

My eyes scanned the screen. I clicked on Reset Your Password.

A new screen appeared.

Enter Old Password: _____
Enter New Password: _____
Confirm New Password: _____

AAAACCKKKK! How could I reset a password if I didn't know the old password? Lost Your Password? it asked me. Yes! I clicked. It asked me a series of security questions. I didn't know any of the answers because, of course, Dana had set them up.

✧19✧

MY PANICKED HEART

I WOKE UP at my desk with my fingers on the keyboard, drool on my chin.

"Go to bed," I said out loud.

I couldn't bring myself to look at the screen again. I shut off the computer, crawled under the covers, and mumbled, "I can fix this. All I need is the password. I'll get it tomorrow first thing and come home and it'll be over."

I was still awake at midnight, telling myself, *I can fix this*, over and over again. At 2:00 a.m. I was trying to figure out how I would get home from school in the middle of the morning without a bus, and what would happen when I didn't show up in my classes. Would they call my mother? By 4:00 a.m. I had decided it would be less noticeable if I stayed at school all day and fixed it as soon as I got home.

At 5:00 a.m. I got up and got dressed and sat on the edge of my bed like a nervous bird in a cage, listening for sounds in the rest of the house.

"You're up so early," Dad said when I walked into the kitchen at six thirty.

"I know. I couldn't sleep anymore, so I thought I'd get dressed."

"I'm about to leave," he said. "Do you want a ride to school?"

"I do!" I would ambush Dana as soon as she got there.

Dad was quiet in the car.

I could see the wheels of worry turning in his head. "It'll be okay, Dad. I'm sure you're not losing your job."

He smiled at me. "You're a good kid, Iris. Thank you. We'll see. I hope not. It has to be some mix-up."

I kept swallowing over and over. I wanted to tell him I was not a good kid, and that I had let a rotten friend do this to him, to our family. I was sure now that she'd done it Monday night while I was only a few feet away doing homework like a dope. She had the password and she was setting a bomb in my family's life. All because she wanted to fly to Chicago instead of taking the bus. This wasn't my fault, but I was going to fix it.

I jumped out of the car in front of school and waved

weakly at Dad. He gripped the wheel and stared straight ahead as he drove away.

There was an early eeriness about the school. Teachers were arriving and talking in the hallways. I'd never heard that before. I felt like I shouldn't be hearing their conversations.

"Who do you have your mortgage with?"

"First Concord. Why? You looking?"

"I'm trying to refinance. Rates are going down . . ."

I wondered if my parents talked to other teachers about stuff like that when the students weren't around.

I kept moving. Straight to Dana's locker. I figured she'd go there first. I leaned against the wall across the hall.

The early bell rang, and buses began arriving. As a sea of kids flooded into the school, their noise buzzed in my ears like static.

She'd arrive soon and I'd confront her. I'd demand the password. I wouldn't even ask why she had done it, because I knew and it didn't matter. I needed that password. That was all I needed.

Ten minutes went by. Twenty minutes. Thirty minutes and the late bell sounded.

No Dana.

I ran to her homeroom and looked through the glass door. She wasn't in her seat.

I headed to the office. "Is Dana Dean sick today?" I asked the school secretary, who knew my mom.

"Hi, Iris. Let me check." She consulted her computer. She clicked and scrolled. "Dana is absent today. You better get to your homeroom."

I wanted to race to her house. But it was too far without my bike. I was going to have to live through the entire day like this.

When I opened the door to my homeroom, I expected to be scolded for being late. Mr. Jaynes looked at me and just nodded toward my desk. From the corner of my eye, I scanned the room. Not one kid raised their head to look at me.

In that moment, POW! It hit me. Everyone in school knew. And I knew exactly how they had found out: They had heard about *Stars in Cars* and googled me, and the site had come up.

And they'd told their friends, who'd told their friends, who'd told their friends.

Ms. Wells had probably told all the teachers—in a nice way. It had spread like wildfire. Yes. They all must know. I was having a meltdown. *Calm down,* I told myself.

The bell rang and my homeroom emptied. I left last, thinking I would avoid the looks.

Outside the door, kids were waiting for me. Four, to be exact. Callie, Bethany, Paige, and Salima crowded together.

"Iris, we saw the Community Bulletin Board post and the fundraising thing," said Callie.

A cloud of even greater confusion descended on my brain. "What Community Bulletin Board post?" I asked with the smallest voice I'd ever heard come out of my mouth.

Bethany pulled out her phone and showed me a page from our local community chat forum. There it was—a post labeled "Help a Local Family" with a link to my page on the "What's Your Dream?" site.

"We wanted to give you something just from us," she said.

My mouth couldn't open. It was clamped shut from shock.

Salima handed me a pink envelope covered with hearts and doodles and glitter, from all four of them. "It has gift certificates for sleepovers at our houses."

My hand trembled as I accepted this crazy-kind gesture. A little moan slipped out of my lips.

"That's okay," said Paige. "You don't have to say anything now. Just let us know."

They looked like they wanted to all reach for a hug, but I stepped back and mumbled, "Thank you."

Then Callie said, "We wanted you to know that we're quitting the Official Lola Bay Fan Club after we get back from the concert tomorrow night. Melanie is too mean and bossy."

"But we didn't want to miss the meet and greet with Lola Bay," said Paige with a sad smile.

I turned and walked through the emptying hallway, watching my feet. I had been given the best friendship gift you could give someone who really lived in a car. I wanted to hand them over to a kid who was actually deserving. That thought made me feel twice as bad. And did Paige say they were going to a meet and greet with Lola Bay?

A teacher came up behind me and put her hand on my shoulder. "Better get to class, honey."

Honey? Oh boy. I walked in a daze through the rest of the morning. Lots more teachers called me honey and said "Bless your heart."

My parents must have known about it by now. How could they not? Even if they didn't read the Community Bulletin Board, someone would have told them. All the teachers at the high school must have been saying *Bless your heart* to my mom. Ugh. My head rolled back. The agony.

I tried to concentrate, but it was hopeless. I hated being a fake poor person. I wasn't having cold nights and an empty stomach. I had won *Stars in Cars*!!!!

Between classes, kids moved around me like water

around a stone in a creek. They thought I was a curiosity. I knew I was pathetic.

Leeza waved at me from down the hall three times as we came close to crossing paths. Her smile was so sad. On the way home, she sat quietly next to me on the bus and looked at her phone. Every few blocks, she'd lean her shoulder into mine and say, "Rah."

Dante, the Goth guy, sang a Lola Bay song and pulled my hair. I barely noticed. I shook my head, trying to get my thoughts straight. I needed to get to Dana's and drag the password out of her.

I dumped my backpack and grabbed my bike.

I wondered what would happen when I took the horrible paragraph down. Maybe I should take the whole page down?

I pumped my bike harder up the hill. With every push of my legs my chest tightened.

What would happen to the money that was in there if I shut down the page?

I huffed and puffed on the slope.

Wait. If I took the whole site down, and I lost all the money, how would I pay my parents for the tickets?

Dana's house came into view. The beat-up old pickup was in the driveway.

My heart pounded as I rang the bell. When nothing happened, I knocked on the door. When still nothing happened, my anger burst through my fists and I slammed them over and over against the door.

The latch clicked, and the door opened with a suction sound. Dana's dad yawned and scratched his chin. "Are we on fire?"

I realized I'd woken him up. "I'm sorry, but I've got to talk to Dana. It's important."

Mr. Dean stepped back and opened the door wider. "Well, I guess you better come in, then."

20

AN ATTEMPTED RECKONING

I RAN DOWN the stairs to her room.

Mr. Dean barked out, "DANA! You got company!"

My hand was hot and sweaty when I grabbed the doorknob. I could hear Lola Bay singing "Thorn in My Soul."

I knocked as I threw open the door. Dana was lying on her bed, flipping through one of the library donation magazines. Her legs were straight and crossed at the ankle. "You woke up my dad. There'll be hell to pay for that."

I didn't care one bit about waking up her dad. "Why weren't you in school?"

"I knew you would be mad."

"I can't believe you did that."

"We needed more money for airplane tickets, that's why."

"Not like that!"

She rolled her eyes. "So take it down. I figured that's what you'd do, anyway."

"I can't take it down because I don't have the password. Give me the password, Dana."

More magazine page flipping. "It's on your desk, dork."

"No, it's not—I looked. And stop calling me dork."

"Well, it's there. I left it there."

"*Well*, no, it's not. You must remember it. Tell me what it is."

"I can't remember it. It was random. One of those long, crazy letter-number things the computer makes up. I think it started with a *T*."

I wanted to run across the room and pound on her head. "You're lying." I spit the words out. "The whole school thinks my family is going to live in a car."

"That's kind of funny."

"It is not funny. Because of it, I got sleepover coupons from Callie, Bethany, Paige, and Salima. Like I have no place to sleep."

"Calm down, Iris. Your family is not moving into a car."

"I KNOW! Give me the password so I can take it down

before my parents see it. We're getting diapers and tuna casserole at our front door. My dad thinks he's really going to lose his job."

"Haven't they seen the Community Bulletin Board?"

I had to stop and think. "Did you do that too?"

"Sure, on Wednesday. You have to do the full range of social media to get to the most people. We needed more money."

I could not believe what I was hearing.

"It's on your desk. Let's go to your house and I'll find it."

"No way!"

Dana yanked on her boots as she talked. "What? Now I'm not your friend?" There was anger in her eyes.

"Yes. You are not my friend anymore." I was almost yelling.

Dana's father's voice boomed down the stairs and I jumped. "I'm trying to sleep up here. Keep it down!"

"Come on. Let's go to your house." Dana stood up.

"You're not coming to my house ever again. I can't trust you." I was breathing so hard, I nearly choked. "Come on. Give me the password."

"What about me, Iris? Can I trust you? Are you going to tell your parents I put up the post?"

My face was on fire. "But you did put it up! And you won't give me the password."

"QUIET!" Dana's dad yelled.

I turned to run up the stairs, and she bolted across the room and grabbed my arm. "But you said I could trust you, Iris. Right?"

I jerked my arm away from her grip. "What do you mean?"

"My mom. She'll go ape squirts if she finds out I've been on your computer." She stepped between me and the door. "I'm sorry. I shouldn't have done it. I only did it so we could fly. I knew I shouldn't have done it as soon as I got home. I thought you would see it and take it down right away and no one would know." Her eyes were pleading. Her perfect hair was a mess. "I left the password on a sticky on your desk. Really!"

"Everyone knows about it now, Dana!"

I pushed past her in a blur, ran out of the house, and jumped on my bike. The pedal scraped deeply into my shin.

Pure adrenaline propelled me home.

Why should I not tell on her?

I could feel blood running down my leg into my shoe.

She's the one who did all of this.

I pushed the pedals in a frenzy. I needed to get home and somehow shut down the page.

As I rounded the last corner, I slowed. Both of our cars were parked in front of the house. That wasn't normal.

I dumped my bike and ran up the porch steps, planning to race up the stairs to my room.

When I opened the door, I knew my parents had found out.

Dad was standing right there, and his face was red.

I didn't say anything. I sat down on the sofa and hung my head. My shoulders couldn't curl any more forward.

"We should wait for your mother," he said. "She's upstairs getting some tissues."

They'd never really yelled at me before, and I felt pretty sure they wouldn't now. Instead, they would be so mega-disappointed, it would be worse than shouting.

Mom walked down the stairs. "Iris. There you are."

It was eerie. Not a *you are the worst child in the world* tone of voice at all. More like a *whose child are you?* voice. My breathing slowed. I was itching to get upstairs and search for the password and take down the post so I could make it all better.

Mom sat down on the edge of the sofa and looked me in the eyes.

I held my breath.

The living room seemed to fill with a buzz that blocked my ability to track the conversation. My mind was splintering in so many bad-for-Iris directions. I didn't say anything. I couldn't.

"We saw the Community Bulletin Board post."

I nodded.

"And the website." Mom sighed a giant sigh. "We think we understand why you did this. You wanted so desperately to go to the concert." She stopped and looked at Dad, then continued in an icy-cold voice. "Before we address the consequences, you have to take the post down." She looked toward the coffee table, where I realized my laptop lay.

"I want to" was all I could get out.

"Go ahead," said Dad in a similar robotic voice.

"I need the password, and it's upstairs."

"Well," Mom said, "go get it."

I jumped up and raced up the stairs to my room.

My hands touched every surface of my desk, every book, every notebook, every stack of papers. I flipped over pencil cups and clips. I shoved things around in search of that scrap of paper. Nothing. I pulled open all the drawers and dumped them. Nothing. I got down on my hands and knees and felt around on the floor, under the wastebasket, behind the curtains, under the bed, in the closet. Nothing. Was this some kind of sick game Dana was playing?

"IRIS!" Dad called from downstairs.

From the top of the stairs I said, "I can't find it."

"Don't you remember it?" Mom yelled.

"No. It's one of those random automatic things."

She said, "Come down here."

Dad picked up the computer. "Let's try to recover it."

The three of us sat on the sofa with me in the middle holding the laptop and them wedging me in.

I powered up the computer and navigated to the site.

The golden bucket was splashing stars and rainbows. Coins were dropping one after the other. The total was $26,015. I gasped.

"Okay," said Dad as if to calm himself. "Get on with it."

I must have been taking too long, because he reached over and took the computer from me. Sweat appeared on his upper lip. He found my account page and clicked on Security. It asked for the password.

After a minute, he found a window that said Forgot Your Password. Up popped the secret questions. He read them out loud. "What is the name of your dog who died?"

I looked at him blankly. He knew I'd never had a dog that died.

"Where were you born?" Dad breathed a sigh of relief like at least he knew that answer. He typed in Minneapolis. **Wrong answer** popped up. **Try again.** He typed in Minnesota. **Wrong answer. Try again.** He looked at me like he expected me to give him the answer.

"I don't know." I hadn't filled it in.

He typed in Fairview Hospital. **Third attempt. Access denied.**

He cursed.

I jumped. I thought he was going to throw the computer against the wall. I put my arms over my head. He got up fast and paced in front of us.

"Why don't you know the answers to the security questions?" he demanded.

My small voice was back. "Because I didn't fill it out."

"Who filled it out?" he asked.

"Dana."

"Why am I not surprised by this," Mom said. She pushed herself off the couch and went into the kitchen. "I need some aspirin."

Dad was back on the computer, this time on the internet typing, *how to recover a password when you don't know the security questions?*

He scrolled and read and scrolled and read. Until finally, he said, "Okay. Let's go back to the site." Once we were on my account page, he scrolled up and down until he found a place to ask for a security code to be texted to my phone.

"Have you got your phone?"

"Yes." I grabbed my backpack.

"Here we go." He made the request and we waited.

It seemed forever until an alert pinged.

"Just hand it to me," Dad said. He read the text, put the code into the box on the screen, and pressed Enter.

In seconds the account was unlocked and all three of us breathed a huge sigh of relief. He reset the password.

"All right, now go to the post and delete it," Dad directed me.

I click, click, clicked.

Mom clamped her hand over her mouth, but a whimper escaped.

My picture, my big fat plea for help, stared at us. The golden bucket glowed, swished, sparkled, clinked, and right there in front of us grew by $10.

They both groaned and shook their heads.

I pressed the Edit icon and put the cursor at the beginning. I wasn't sure what to write.

"Delete the whole post, save it, and close it for now," said Dad.

"Should she delete the entire account?" Mom asked him. "What should we do about all that money?"

"No!" I stood up and turned to face them. "Please listen. Okay? I've made a million mistakes and I am sorry for all of them and I'll tell you every one of them and do anything you want, but please listen. That bad post only went up on Monday night. Up until then, all the donations were fair. They were for me to go to the concert. No lies. I'm begging you. Please." My hands were stretched into fists, and tears were squirting out of my eyes. I slunk to my knees.

"Oh, goodness, get up, Iris," said Mom. "Don't be so dramatic." She was mad, but I could tell she had some sympathy for my anguish.

"Let's just delete this post, save it, and close it. Then we'll have a talk," said Dad.

I sobbed. "Thank you!"

He closed the computer.

Mom started in. "So, did you put up the post because you wanted to go to the concert or because you thought Dad was losing his job?"

"No!!!!" I wailed.

"Let her talk, Marnie. From the beginning, Iris," said Dad.

From the beginning? That was almost too much to tell. But I had my chance to make this last thing right. "No. I didn't do it. I didn't think Dad was losing his job. Dana made that up and I didn't know."

Mom threw her hands up in frustration. "Why?"

"Okay. Okay. Listen. It all kind of started when they announced that Lola Bay was having concert dates in Chicago, and Dana and I wanted to get tickets, so we borrowed your credit card to buy the tickets for $300."

Mom's face turned red so fast, I thought steam would shoot out of her ears, but Dad put his hand on hers to calm her.

"Wait. Please. It was just borrowing. And I know it

was wrong and I shouldn't have done it. But you asked me if I wanted your credit card for pizza, so you must have trusted me once with the card. But then I was bugging Dana about how we were going to pay you back, and she came up with this website we could post on. And I figured if someone could get money for a three-legged dog to swim, I could get contributions to go to a concert in Chicago. And it was all okay until we figured out that rather than taking a bus, we might need to fly and would need more money because of *Stars in Cars* being here in Minneapolis in the morning. So without telling me, Dana put that awful lie up to raise more money." I stopped to take a breath. "And she's very sorry, but I didn't accept her apology."

"When were you planning to go to Chicago?" Mom asked. "And what about a three-legged dog?"

"This Saturday," I said. "After *Stars in Cars*."

"Tomorrow?" she asked like she didn't understand. "And you were going to take an airplane?"

"Mr. Dean was going to take us because he is a musician and he understands our passion for Lola Bay."

Dad moved around in his seat. "Hang on. Dana's father is planning to take you both to Chicago tomorrow? Was anyone going to ask us about this?"

"No. He's not. I don't even know if Dana has asked

him yet. That was just her idea. But we needed money for the trip if he said yes."

"Okay. Stop. Where does the money from the website go?" Mom asked.

"That's just it. It all goes to your credit card."

"Oh my God," Dad said.

"Don't swear, Charles," said Mom.

"Oh my holy Hercules. How's that, Marnie? All that money that was raised under false pretenses is going to our credit card. We need to stop that right now and get those contributions reversed."

"The money up to Monday night was fair. I need it to pay back your card for the concert tickets. We can give all the rest back." I felt for sure I was being helpful.

"Iris, you are not entitled to any of this money," said Dad. "You're not old enough to be on that site. It will have to be shut down as soon as we are finished here, and all that money returned. None of it can go to our credit card. We'll just pay the credit card bill and you will find a way to pay us back. Understand?"

I nodded.

Mom stared out the front window. "What a mess. I can't quite believe you did this, Iris."

I sat on the floor and pulled my knees up close to my body. "I know. I'm so, so sorry. I completely goofed up."

Then she said to no one in particular, "That Dana."

"Dana's sorry too, and if her mom finds out, she will be in way worse trouble than I am."

"What does that mean?" asked Dad.

"She's not allowed to be online because she abuses her online privileges. She's good at, you know, the internet. So she broke the rule her mom made that she can't be online except supervised for school." I looked at Mom. "I know you don't like Dana."

"You are right this time. I don't like Dana one stinking little bit."

Oh, this was hard. I looked at Dad. "And I know there is stuff that is water under the bridge that can't be fixed. Like Ian writing in my math book."

"This is way bigger than that, Iris." He swallowed hard. "Okay. Did she do anything else on your computer?"

"Not really. She pretended to check out library books at the school library, and she ordered Lola Bay Fan Club swag."

Dad and Mom both relaxed a teensy bit.

"And she used my phone to hack into Melanie Fisher's phone and send a mean text that started a fight between Melanie and her friends. And Melanie Fisher might be able to figure out it came from my phone."

Mom shook her head and sighed.

I paused.

"What else?" Dad asked.

"That's it."

They both looked at the computer as if it were suddenly a distasteful problem object in the house.

Mom said, "Iris, I think we need to check your browser history to see where Dana has gone on your computer. I know it will have your personal history too, but I'd like your okay to do that. Do you understand why?"

I could hardly believe she was actually asking for my permission. "Yeah, sure. That's okay."

"And regardless of what we find, we'll have to tell her parents about all of this. They should also know about the library, the merch, the website posting, and the credit card. There has to be some accountability so she doesn't do this to another child—to another family."

I winced at being called a child. But I knew it had to be done. I nodded.

My phone chimed that a text had arrived.

It was from Sam from *Stars in Cars*.

> Iris and Mr. and Mrs. Underwood. I am Iris's handler tomorrow. Samantha Nguyen. I am with the Lola Bay logistics team. I will meet you at the East Security Gate at the Target Center at 8 a.m. It's going to be great!

In snapped us all into the reality that life was moving on at a hundred miles an hour.

The last thing Mom said to me that night was, "Sometime when this is all over, you can explain about swimming lessons for the three-legged dog."

My bed did not bring sleep. All it held was the agony of wondering whether Lola Bay knew about my awful post. Should I tell her? Or should I not say anything because it was all going to go away? What if she had seen it? What if she hadn't seen it and didn't know a thing about it? I'd asked Mom and Dad if they thought I should tell her, and they'd both said after a long silence that I would have to make that choice.

21

STARS IN CARS

KDQB WAS BROADCASTING over giant loudspeakers. "Ladies and gentlemen, after this commercial break, we'll return with twelve-year-old Iris Underwood, who is waiting for her chance of a lifetime to ride and sing in a car with rock star Lola Bay."

The temperature had dropped to biting cold. I stood in front of the main entrance to the Target Center in Minneapolis with Sam. TV reporters and cameramen hovered nearby as we waited for the limo carrying Lola Bay to pull up. Leeza, Regina, Ted, and Robert stood behind a barrier. Leeza hopped from foot to foot and waved at me.

"How you doing, kid?" One of the reporters nudged me. "Big day, huh?"

I pulled and pushed my Lola Bay PopSocket on the back of my phone. Lola Bay's press woman, Sam, tried to stay between me and the reporters to keep them from bothering me. She talked on her phone as she leaned into the street, watching for the car. She looked a little stressed. That may have been her permanent face.

I reminded myself to take selfies with Lola Bay. *Remember to take selfies, remember to take selfies,* I repeated in my head. I figured I might melt when I finally saw her in the flesh and sat in a car with her. I imagined she'd be super-sweet.

The corner of North Sixth Street and North First Avenue was blocked off from traffic, and the sidewalk was filled with bundled-up kids singing along and dancing to blasting Lola Bay music. Kids from my class, kids from my school, kids from all over the Twin Cities. All waiting to see me get into a car with Lola Bay.

Pop and push. Any minute now Lola Bay would take me for a ride around the city in the red car sitting on a trailer next to me. Sam explained to me that Lola Bay would look like she was driving, and I'd be next to her, but we'd be pulled by a truck. The car had a camera inside, and we would be singing her songs. It would be all over the internet and YouTube and Instagram and whatever.

I scanned for my parents. There they were—near Leeza.

Camera shutters clicked in bursts.

I hopped back and forth.

Sam said, "If you have to go to the bathroom, sorry. It's too late. You'll have to hold it."

"No. I'm okay." I curled my fingers inside my mittens. My right cheek itched. I wanted to scratch it, but I did what Carl, Lola Bay's makeup man, had said: Don't touch—don't smudge.

The song switched from "I See You" to "Willing to Believe," and the volume increased. I panicked and couldn't remember what I was wearing. I looked down. They weren't the clothes Mom and I had picked out. We'd called them my *Stars in Cars* clothes. But the costume man (who was also Carl) had screamed, "I don't think so!"

I was now wearing jeans and a baggy neon blue jacket. He had wanted to spray my hair with apple green, but I refused. Even though I liked that Lola Bay had different hair all the time. Different colors, styles, and cuts. It was great on her but not me.

Sam was back. "Don't move," she told me, and got back on her phone. "Ready here." She paused and looked at her phone as if it had stopped working. "Sorry, say that again?"

I told myself I didn't need to go to the bathroom.

A blast of wind whipped across the street, and I covered my ears with my mittens. My nose was running. I wiped it with my sleeve. A mass scream rolled down the street. Sam perched on the curb and waved her arm high and wide.

TV and radio people talked into their microphones. Cameras were lifted.

Something tickled in my throat. It felt like a hairball.

A giant black stretch limo inched around the corner.

Screaming and more screaming filled the cold air.

I squeezed my knees together. I really, really needed to pee.

Sam's hands on my back pushed me toward the curb.

My legs felt numb. I hoped my mouth wasn't hanging open. I looked at my parents. Dad gave me a thumbs-up. I tried to feel my feet against the concrete.

A crush of kids bumped against a barrier, tipping it over, and they were motioned back.

The car loomed in front of me. Sam waved to me. "COME HERE."

She opened the back door and leaned in. Her leather jacket was short, and her tee underneath had ostriches on it.

This made me giggle. I didn't mean to laugh but it kind of slipped out. This was insanity.

Yesterday, the world was crashing down around me, and now I was about to meet Lola Bay and sing with her in a fake car.

I no longer needed to pee. Funny how that worked—mind over matter—fear over bladder.

Screaming on the street hurt my ears. Sam backed out of the car and waved at me with her phone. Her mouth moved. "Lola wants to talk to you—in the car." She held the door open.

I took a deep breath.

I was about to have the best time of my life.

My coat got caught in the door, and Sam had to shut it twice. Even though it was toasty warm inside, I tugged the neon blue coat around me like a security blanket. My breath caught and I felt like my mind was going to escape my skull and float out of my body. I tried to focus. Lola Bay was all a blur at first. Then she came clear in my vision.

She was a person. A real person. A girl. An older girl.

For sure, she was dressed like a glowing yellow canary. She had a jeweled phone in her hand, and her bird-like wrist pointed it at her face. Her heart-shaped lips were reading a text as she scrolled.

I waited.

She glanced up.

"Hey. Iris. How's it going?" Her voice was casual, and she tipped her head in a friendly way.

My voice cracked, and I made a squeaky noise as I tried to say, "Fine."

She softened even more. "Hey, you don't have to put

on a good face. I know it must really suck." My body went numb. I watched her mouth move. "You know, my family wasn't rich or anything. We had this little house and, like, one car."

"Oh yeah?" Little house. One car.

She must know.

"Yep. Totally," she said. "I had to wear my annoying sister Mona's jeans. Can you believe it?"

"Wow. No."

She reached to hug me, and I leaned back and tears gushed from my eyes like a fire hydrant.

"Oh, kiddo. Really, it's okay." She dug in her giant handbag and pulled out tissues. "You can be cool with me. I love what you wrote about my music. It was the best. And then when Sam showed me that your family is having trouble, well. I thought it was meant to be that I picked your entry. I didn't even know. Can you believe that!"

Tears streamed down my face. I struggled not to make eye contact, but I couldn't help myself.

"What's wrong?"

My voice choked out a strangled confession. "It's not true."

"What's not true?"

"It's made-up."

"What's made-up? Didn't you write your own entry— that line about my music mending your heart?"

I nodded yes about fifty times. "Yes, I did write it. That's totally mine."

Then I saw it: a giant cardboard check for $50,000 by her feet made out to the Underwood Family. She put her hand on it. "It's going to be okay. Calm down. I'm presenting this to you and your family today."

I groaned and sucked snot into my throat. "Lola Bay, I love you. You are my favorite singer in the whole world. You are my biggest fan. But you can't give us that check."

She laughed a little. "Okay, *I* am *your* biggest fan, huh? I get that, but why can't I help your family? Why not?"

I turned and faced her square-on. This was my moment of complete truth. "Because what was on the internet about my family being homeless isn't true."

"What! Oh man. You mean you're not going to live in a car?" She squinted and shook her head like she was trying to absorb what I'd said. "Why would you put that up if it wasn't true?"

"I didn't do it. My friend did it. She was trying to raise money so we could fly to Chicago for the concert tonight. I didn't know she did it."

She threw her head back against the seat. "What the heck! You better get new friends, kid!"

A new wave of tears washed over me. I wiped makeup all over my blue sleeve. "I'm soooo, soooo sorry."

Her voice sharpened. "I can't do this car thing with you."

I could barely talk. "Why not? I won the contest."

She looked around the inside of the limo like she was trying to find a way out of this situation. "This is a major screwup, Iris Underwood."

"I know."

"You're in a real mess, you know."

"I know. I know."

"Obviously, I can't give you the check. The whole world knows you had that homeless story out there. We had a whole press packet ready to launch on helping your family. I even wrote a song, 'Mend My Heart,' that was going to debut today. Damn. I'll see if I can hold it. If I do this with you now, it'll look like you scammed me."

"But I didn't. I took it down as soon as I knew—as soon as I could."

She rolled her eyes in disbelief. "Don't you get it? Stuff on the internet never goes away. How old are you?"

"Twelve."

She put her palms against her eyes like she was thinking hard. Several seconds passed, and then she leaned forward and moaned. I didn't move. Several more seconds passed.

Suddenly, Lola Bay sat up and took a deep cleansing breath. "Listen, Iris. This is bad, but it's not the freakin' end of the world. So don't go getting scarred for life or anything, okay? It's not like I haven't had some major screwups." She bounced her phone in her hand. "The good thing is that I didn't get dragged into it. I mean, we didn't do the ride, which would have haunted us both. And I didn't give you the check, which would have been a whole other nightmare. We can get out of this."

I sucked up more snot. "I know you don't have any friends who would treat you this way, because you are Lola Bay."

"Oh, puh-leeze, Iris. It's fifty times worse for me. I'm a magnet for users and losers."

She pressed her fingertips into the corners of her eyes, being careful not to mess up her makeup. "Look. I had some real hard learning experiences with rotten friends. One for sure that I will never forget or forgive. And believe me, you won't forget this one. You know Taylor Swift, right? It's like Taylor says, you've got to shake it off and not let it happen again. Get it? Shake it off."

I whispered, "I do. Thanks."

"Now get out. I have to call my manager and delay that song's release."

"Okay."

She powered down the window and Sam's face appeared. "Tell them the car's camera isn't working and we're headed back to the airport."

Sam didn't blink. "Got it."

She opened the car door and took one look at me and whispered, "Go into the Target Center and head into the ladies' room where we did your makeup. I'll send Carl in to clean you up."

I didn't look right or left. I put my head down and ran.

When I got to the bathroom, I slammed through the door of the first stall and barfed into the toilet.

22

FACE IT

TWO MINUTES LATER, the bathroom door banged open. I assumed it was Carl. I wiped my mouth with toilet paper and was about to come out of the stall when I heard Dana's voice.

"Are you in here, Iris?"

Oh my gosh, of course she'd be here this morning, probably hoping to meet Lola Bay. But I really didn't need her stalking me right now.

"Go away."

"What did you do, Iris?" Dana cried. "Did you tell Lola Bay?" She slammed her hand against the door. "You really are the worst friend in the history of the world!

Don't you know what this means? Now everyone will know I did it. My mom will know I did it." She didn't wait for me to answer. "And I was so nice to you. I was your friend when Melanie Fish Face stole the club. I gave you bracelets that I made myself. And you're a sixth grader, even. I hung out with you and did Lola Bay stuff when that loser Leeza wouldn't do it anymore. And I said I was sorry. And I didn't mean for it to get like this."

That was it. I screamed, "Leeza is not a loser, and she can do whatever she wants! You and I were friends because of Lola Bay, not because of Leeza. And saying you're sorry doesn't make it go away!"

She pounded on my stall door. "Come out!"

I pounded on the other side. My face felt hot and swollen. I wanted to throw open the door and flail my arms at her like the twins did when they were in a knock-down, drag-out fight. But I steadied myself on the sides of the stall. I tried to get my voice down, but it was no use. It wanted to yell. "You only wanted to be my friend so you could use my computer, so you could mess around with it because you think you're so smart. That's not being a friend."

I put my hand up to my throat. It hurt from yelling. The bathroom door opened again.

"Iris?" It was Carl.

I opened the stall door.

He took one look at us and backed out.

Spit flew out with my next words. "You are a liar. You put up a lie about my family and wanted me to take the blame for it, but I told my parents the truth. And yes, I told Lola Bay the truth about the homeless lie. I told her I didn't do it." I was breathing hard now, but I had one more thing to say to her. "And guess what? I'm shaking you off."

She went ghostly white. Right then my parents pushed open the bathroom door.

Mom zeroed in on the tension. "Iris, what's going on?"

Dana rushed past them.

"Let's go home," I said to my parents. "I want to go home now."

✦✦✦

In the car, Mom said, "What did Dana say to you in the bathroom?"

I thought about the yelling through the stall door. "Nothing that mattered."

She continued, "What a shame the car ride was canceled."

Dad said, "Tough break."

I took a huge breath and said, "What did they tell all the people?"

Dad looked at me in the rearview mirror with a wrinkled brow. "That there was a problem with cameras. Why? What did they tell you?"

"That's right. That's what they told me too."

"On the bright side," he said, "now we can all go to the Greek festival."

For the rest of the ride home, I stared out the window and thought about Lola Bay.

I met Lola Bay. I sat in a car with her and was happy with her. I cried in front of her. She was mad at me, but she was decent to me. She was probably nicer than she had to be.

I wished so hard that she didn't have to know about the lie on the internet. The internet sucked so bad. I hated the internet.

I was proud that she'd written a song about my prize-winning entry, even if no one would ever know that now. I hoped the song would come out sometime. I would know. She would know that I would know. I'd always be her very special, unusual circumstances fan.

With my stomach full of souvlaki, I sprawled out flat on my back on my bed and stared at the ceiling.

Mom knocked and said, "Leeza is here."

Leeza fell down on the bed next to me but didn't say anything.

I studied the drum-shaped light fixture I'd picked out. It looked dusty. There were cracks in the plaster around it.

Leeza nudged me with her arm. "What the rah, Iris? What in the world is going on?"

"Dana and I aren't friends anymore."

"Yeah. I got that. She was bah. Can't say I'm sad."

"Okay, shut up about that. I know."

"Okay."

"We're not going to be homeless."

"Everybody figured that, since you took the page down, so that's good."

I sat up. "Really? Is that what people think? At school? And everywhere?"

"Sure. We all figured that your dad didn't lose his job, so it was all okay. And my mom got a notice that her contribution was being returned, so, cool."

I needed to absorb this. To think it through. This was a completely unexpected development. Maybe no one was blaming me for lying. They simply thought the bad thing didn't happen and they were getting their contributions back. I could see Lola Bay's mouth moving as she was saying, *Shake it off*.

We didn't talk for a while.

Finally, Leeza said, "I'm glad you were never going to be homeless. That would have been bah."

"I know."

She hugged the pillow. "My parents were going to ask your family if you wanted to move in with us."

"Really?"

"You could have stayed in my room."

We went quiet for a long time.

Until Leeza said, "Do you want to come to practice Monday? Do you want to play?"

I laughed. "No!"

"I'm not kidding. You would be good at it."

"I'm not kidding either. Why would I want to punch a snowman's head?"

Leeza pinched me.

"Ouch!"

"Seriously. You'd have a team. It's cool."

I imagined myself clowning around, missing the ball, bonking people in the head, and yelling *Sorry* all the time. "I don't think I'm the team type."

"We've always been a team," said Leeza.

"Yeah. I guess. A team of rainbow unicorns."

But we both knew it was different now. We were older. We'd changed. We both knew so much more about so many things.

"You want to go to this place tomorrow with me and my family?"

"What place?"

"It's supposed to be really good. It's called Monkey Don Donuts."

23
ONWARD

DANA WASN'T IN school on Monday. Most kids ignored me. Some said, "Too bad about the car."

I turned a corner and Melanie Fish Face and the entire gang of Imitators were blocking my way. They were all hugging their books. I adjusted my backpack over my shoulder and made a move around them.

"Iris. Too bad you didn't get to ride with Lola Bay."

"Yeah, too bad."

"The concert was incredible."

"Good," I said, like of course it would be.

"So," Melanie said, then paused. "If you want to be official, I guess you can, since you met Lola Bay and all."

She stuck her hand out with an Official Lola Bay Fan Club card with my name on it. It was signed by her.

Almost automatically, I took the card. Did I even deserve to be in the Official Lola Bay Fan Club? Why, oh why did Melanie have to be the door between me and the club? But what good was an unofficial club of me and me alone?

"You can tell us all about meeting her," Melanie said in a conspiratorial way, like she was going to get all the secrets of being with Lola Bay and be able to claim them as her own.

I stood there, looking at the whole gang of them. I had no intention of telling them one single thing about my time with Lola Bay. And in that second I knew I didn't want to be in any club with them either. Before I realized what I was doing, I was handing the card back to her.

"No, thanks," I said.

Melanie's eyes flashed anger, then she instantly shifted her face to pity and shrugged, and she and her minions walked away.

In Studio Arts, Ms. Wells was waiting for me.

She'd rested a big stretched canvas on my easel. A box on the floor held a baggie filled with tubes of paint, a bottle of glue, pens, markers, brushes, clay tools, and a paper bag stuffed with scraps of colored, textured paper, shiny and coarse fabric, leaves and pine needles.

"What's this for?" I reached down and touched bits of it.

"Go ahead. It's hard to resist, I know." She laughed. "You're going to keep working on collage."

I poked around in the bags, feeling sharp and dull, grainy and slick. I glanced at the white canvas, and it seemed impossible that I could compose anything on it. I had nothing left to say. I was empty.

"It's kind of bleak looking, isn't it?" she mused. "A new white canvas always asks the question *Will it be worth it?*"

I ran my hand lightly across the canvas, letting my fingertips touch it here and there. They still had chips of French manicure on them. "I'll probably mess it up. You should use it."

"I've already got a work in progress that I'm messing up all by myself, thank you very much," she said. "No, this is yours to mess up all by yourself."

I knew she was an artist, but until this moment I hadn't thought about her working on her own pieces—and messing them up.

"You know," she said, "collage is the perfect medium for messing up and fixing and moving on. It's my medium too."

"I don't know if I can make anything good."

"It all depends on what you're trying to achieve."

"I'd like to make something beautiful."

"You will."

"You think?"

"Sure. You'll probably hate, and love, and hate, and love what you put here, but it will be beautifully you. Just art-it-out."

I looked over at the empty stool where Dana usually sat and wondered when she would be back and what that would be like. My eyes scanned the room and landed on Robert Benally's easel. He raised a wet paintbrush to me. I raised a small piece of orange velvet back at him.

When the class was almost over, I walked over to him and said, "Hey."

He said, "Hey."

And he showed me all of his art supplies and how he used his brushes to create feathers, and I took him to my easel and shared my collection of leaves and fabric scraps. We talked about the artists we liked and pizza until it was time for the bus.

I merged into the throng in the hallway and moved to the buses. Leeza had practice, so she wouldn't be there.

We bumped along, the driver sticking the red sign out at every stop. The kid noise rocked the walls of the bus, but I barely noticed. I leaned to avoid a flying hat.

Dana was still on my mind, and how she was always giving me chances. I decided the best kind of chance is the one you give yourself.

Ms. Wells was on my mind. She treated me like I was a real artist.

And collage. Collage was on my mind. What was it Ms. Wells had said about messing up and fixing and moving on? That's what I was going to do. I'd art-it-out.

And maybe someday Lola Bay's song "Mend My Heart" would play on the radio, and I would know she remembered me—her very special fan who got all tangled up, then got untangled and learned to shake it off.

Then I slapped my forehead. Had I really told Lola Bay *she* was *my* biggest fan? I sure had. Oh well. It wasn't the biggest, most earth-shattering, life-changing thing I'd done.

⇉ ACKNOWLEDGMENTS ⇇

I have been fortunate to have wonderful professionals, friends, and relatives support me in bringing this story to readers. Thanks to Catherine Frank, Magda Surrisi, my critique partners, and my middle grade beta readers: Ellie Surrisi Camp, Mairi Ling, Annabelle Hamburger, and Ava Weatherford. Huge hugs to my agent, Kelly Dyksterhouse, who is always there to support me with advice and good humor. I am grateful to Jen Klonsky, Ari Lewin, and Susan Kochan for recognizing and sharing in my vision and guiding it to this beautifully styled volume. Thanks to the magnificent Putnam team and the entire Penguin Random House family. Finally, heaps of appreciation for parents, teachers, librarians, and book-sellers. The world is constantly changing, but middle grade complexities and challenges endure. It is a special time, and valuable core skills are being learned. I feel honored to be among the adults who are trying to lend a helping hand.

⇒ ABOUT THE AUTHOR ⇐

C. M. SURRISI has done many jobs, including wildlife tracking device assembler, cook, tap dancer, actor, teacher, and lawyer. She is now a full-time writer, as well as wife, mother, and grandmother. Her interests are wide and diverse and she has written about many of them in picture books, middle grade mysteries, young adult nonfiction, and adult mysteries. She lives in Minnesota with her husband and two cats. She is a voracious reader and has a special place in her heart for middle grade readers and the middle grade experience.